How can the heavens look so perfect when down on Earth my life is so messed up?

"If only I could be like Kate. Or Lisa. Or even Sara," Jamie whispered to the stars. "They know how to talk to boys. How to flirt and get boys to like them."

She closed her eyes tight and wrapped her arms around herself.

Please, she prayed, *please let me change. Let me learn how to flirt.*

She opened her eyes to the stars once more. "It's not really so much to ask, is it?" she said. "I haven't been able to flirt with guys for fifteen years and five months. So now, I'm asking. Could you just give me the flirting gene? So that I can talk to Nick? So that he'll fall in love with me? Please?"

And then she thought: *Funny thing about the stars. Twinkling away up there, they seem to promise everything.*

But they never, ever answer your wish.

Mirror Image books
by Cherie Bennett and Jeff Gottesfeld

Stranger in the Mirror
Rich Girl in the Mirror
Star in the Mirror
Flirt in the Mirror

Flirt in the Mirror

MIRROR IMAGE

Cherie Bennett

and

Jeff Gottesfeld

AN ARCHWAY PAPERBACK
Published by POCKET BOOKS
New York London Toronto Sydney Singapore

This book is a work of fiction. Names, characters, places and incidents are products of the authors' imagination or are used fictitiously. Any resemblance to actual events or locales or persons, living or dead, is entirely coincidental.

AN ARCHWAY PAPERBACK *Original*

An Archway Paperback published by
POCKET BOOKS, a division of Simon & Schuster, Inc.
1230 Avenue of the Americas, New York, NY 10020

Copyright © 2000 by Cherie Bennett and Jeff Gottesfeld

ISBN: 0-671-03633-5

First Archway Paperback printing December 2000

10 9 8 7 6 5 4 3 2 1

AN ARCHWAY PAPERBACK and colophon are registered trademarks of Simon & Schuster, Inc.

Front cover illustration by Kamil Vojnar

Printed in the U.S.A.

IL 5+

for our wonderful editor and friend,
Pat MacDonald

Prologue

⹋

** NATIONAL SECURITY MEMORANDUM #3 **
EXTREME TOP-SECRET, EYES-ONLY,
LIMITED DISTRIBUTION

THIS IS COPY NUMBER 7 OUT OF 15 TOTAL

From: Dr. Louise Warner, Chair, Substance Z project
To: Substance Z Recovery/Field Test Team
Re: Search for Additional Teen Girls in Possession of
    Loverocks

Following the unplanned-for return to Earth of
the top-secret Substance Z satellite developed
by our research team and launched by the
Department of Defense, our unit has been en-

gaged in high-priority monitoring of the general population of the southern United States in an effort to determine whether any ordinary citizens may now possess chunks of that satellite's dangerous payload and may have been subject to the so-called Mirror Image Effect.

This is what we know so far:

a) Our satellite exploded in the atmosphere in early September, over the city of New Orleans, Louisiana.

b) Chunks of Substance Z, exposed to radiation while in orbit, have returned to Earth as a result of the explosion.

c) All chunks recovered so far have assumed a heart-shaped, crystalline structure and are objects of great beauty.

d) We have identified and tracked three teen girls, all age fifteen, who came into possession of chunks of activated Substance Z and underwent the Mirror Image Effect:

1. Callie Bailey, a self-described geeky girl, who became gorgeous after finding her Sub Z;

2. Marilee Ellis, a poor girl who subsequently won the Louisiana Lotto;

3. Sue Lloyd, a stagestruck girl with little acting talent, who became a star actress at her high school.

Each of these girls, we learned, called her chunk of activated Substance Z a "Loverock," probably because of its heart-shaped appearance.

New computer models indicate that several Loverocks may have fallen to earth in or near the community of LaGrange, Louisiana, fifteen miles north of New Orleans. To that end, we are dispatching a special reconnaissance and recovery team to LaGrange to monitor and report on the situation.

One final note: A Loverock has the effect of making the deepest desire of the first person to come in contact with it come true. The effect may be reversible, in some unknown way. While all the subjects so far who have undergone the Mirror Image Effect have been teen girls, this may not be true in the future.

Please exercise extreme caution in dealing with any Loverocks you may find.

DESTROY THIS MEMO AFTER READING.

Chapter

1

"*L*et's play Choose or Lose," Kate McGee suggested, with a wicked glint in her eye.

"I hate that game," Jamie Dobrin groaned. "Besides, we're supposed to be talking about our 'zine. You know? *American Grrls?* We haven't done an issue in four months."

"Forget the 'zine for a minute. What's wrong with Choose or Lose?" Kate popped a handful of popcorn into her mouth.

"I don't know. For one thing, it's mean," Jamie said and sighed.

Lisa Sherwin drew her knees up to her chin and wrapped her arms around them. "Only if you take it seriously, Jam."

"Okay, how about, it's humiliating?" Jamie asked.

"It's just for fun," Sara Torres said softly.

"How come we never work on the 'zine anymore? And how come I always get outvoted about this stupid game?" Jamie grumbled. Still, she was ready to put aside her desire to talk about their 'zine—they'd published it regularly on the Web and in school until about four months ago—and go along with her best friends.

Basically Jamie Dobrin liked her life. She got along with her parents and little brother, and she had the three best friends in the world. It was Saturday night, and these three best friends were at Jamie's house for a sleepover. The next day they'd be going to the French Quarter—the old section of New Orleans where all the best music clubs were— to hear Sara's father play saxophone with his pickup jazz band, The Hot Profs.

I wanted to write about that jazz concert for American Grrls, Jamie thought suddenly. *Oh, well.*

She had also wanted to write about Kate's momentous sixteenth birthday last week. They were all sophomores, but the rest of them were still a few months away from turning sixteen.

But now Kate had turned the magic number—as in, driver's license. As in, her own car, which her parents had given her as a birthday present. Tomorrow would be the first time the four of them would travel alone, not dependent on someone's parents.

Jamie could hardly wait.

"Jam, out of popcorn," Kate said, picking semi-popped kernels out of the bottom of the bowl. "Want me to go make more?"

"I'll go," Jamie said, scrambling to her feet. "The new microwave is kind of temperamental."

" 'Kay." Kate stretched out her long legs and clicked one fuzzy leopard print slipper against the other. "Oh, and can we have some more of those killer chocolate-chip cookies your mom baked?"

"Sure," Jamie said, reaching for the empty popcorn bowl. "You know, they ought to put your metabolism in *The Guinness Book of World Records.* You eat everything in sight and stay skinny."

"She's metabolically blessed," Lisa said.

"True," Kate agreed, leaning back on the palms of her hands. "Want me to help, Jam?"

"I'll go with her," Sara offered quickly, getting up from the lavender carpet.

"You guys just start the game without us," Jamie told them.

"No way." Kate laughed and tossed her long chestnut hair off her face in a sexy new way she'd developed lately. "Choose or Lose is no fun without everyone. We'll wait till you guys get back."

Jamie and Sara headed to the kitchen to the sound of Kate and Lisa's laughter.

The kitchen had just been remodeled, and Jamie still had a hard time remembering where everything was. Her mom was ecstatic over the new kitchen, but frankly, Jamie liked the kitchen better the way it had been before.

Simpler.

She liked her friends better the way they had been before, too.

Simpler.

She rooted around in a cupboard and found a new jumbo bag of popcorn, stuck it into the microwave, and set the temperamental timer for four minutes on High. Sara leaned against the butcher-block counter. "You're not really that upset about playing that stupid game, are you?" she asked.

"Not really," Jamie said. But mostly she said it because it was what Sara wanted her to say.

"Kate's just fooling around," Sara said.

"I know." Jamie began to take cookies out of the ceramic cookie jar and put them on a platter. "It's just . . . well, the four of us didn't used to sit around playing something like Choose or Lose."

Sara looped some of her long, dark hair behind one ear. "Things change. We're not all ten anymore."

"Yeah. I know, but the 'zine is cool. I wrote about music and you wrote about culture and Kate covered fashion and Lisa drew cartoons."

"Like I said, things change, Jamie."

"We got the last issue out, just the two of us," Jamie reminded her friend. "We could do that again."

"Maybe," Sara said noncomittally.

Jamie sighed. Ten. That's how old they were

when they'd become best friends. Actually Kate, who had just moved to LaGrange, the suburb of New Orleans where they lived, had been almost eleven.

To the other girls, she had seemed very worldly and sophisticated. For one thing, she had moved from Malibu, which was this really cool beach town right near Los Angeles where a lot of movie stars lived. For another thing, she had an older sister who told her everything about everything.

Finally, Kate—who was long-legged and daring, with a very cute overbite—was the possessor of a bikini so tiny that none of the other girls' mothers would ever, ever, ever have allowed them to wear it. So what they did was take turns secretly borrowing it from Kate.

• She knew everything about fashion and clothes, so she became the style editor of *American Grrls*. And the four of them had become inseparable.

Kate. And Lisa. Blond-haired, sunny, a great cartoonist, and hopelessly romantic, Lisa sort of worshipped Kate. Like Kate, she started getting a figure way before Jamie and Sara did. And the figure she developed was awesome to behold. So was Kate's, for that matter. It gave both of them major status at school—and lots of attention from guys.

Actually, raven-haired Sara, with her huge dark eyes and heart-shaped face, was the one with whom Jamie felt the closest. Sara's family had immigrated to New Orleans from Mexico when

Sara was a baby, so she had no memory of her birthplace at all. But her parents, both professors at Tulane University, were careful to make sure their kids never forgot their heritage. At home, for example, they spoke English on weekdays and Spanish on weekends.

All the Torres kids were held to the highest standards. In everything. The standards were so tough that two of Sara's older siblings had rebelled in a big way. One had dropped out of college to travel through Europe. The other had quit high school.

But Sara, the youngest, more than made up for their rebellions. She was an amazing writer, and wrote funny and sarcastic articles for *American Grrls* about the perils of growing up at the start of the new millennium. She was one of the top students in her class, always nice, well-mannered, and soft-spoken. Her room was always neat. Her clothes were always perfect. She never cussed or drank or smoked. She called adults "ma'am" and "sir." She even did volunteer work at a homeless shelter.

Sometimes Jamie was in total awe of Sara. She knew she'd freak if her parents ever expected her to be *that* perfect.

Sara was a wonderful friend, though. Jamie knew she could always count on her. Sara really listened. Also, she was the kind of friend who would never reveal a secret or play one friend against another.

That last thing was the most important. Especially lately, when it seemed more and more as if the four best friends were breaking off into two pairs of best friends. Kate and Lisa, who had dropped out of the 'zine. And Sara and Jamie, who tried to keep the 'zine going.

But I won't end a friendship because my friends don't want to work with me on a 'zine anymore, Jamie thought. *Not that there's anything so awful about me,* Jamie assured herself as she emptied the freshly popped corn into the bowl. *I'm a good student. I'm on the soccer team. I love music of all kinds—not just hip-hop, but jazz and classical, and even sometimes opera. I'm not horrible looking or anything. Everyone says I have great hair. And I did luck out and inherit my mom's green eyes. But I could never be as audacious as Kate. Or as curvy and cute as Lisa. Or as perfect as Sara.*

Most of the time I feel like I'm just . . . there.

"You off in another galaxy?" Sara asked, breaking into Jamie's thoughts.

"Yeah, kinda," she admitted. Then she sighed. "So, are you ready to play this game that neither of us wants to play?"

"I don't mind, I told you," Sara said. She picked up the platter of cookies and they headed for the stairs. "I think it's kind of fun."

"Since when?" Jamie demanded. "I thought you were just being nice before. You hate Choose or Lose."

Sara shrugged her graceful shoulders but didn't answer.

Jamie knew it was stupid, but that shrug made her feel terrible. Because Choose or Lose was always about guys—who liked whom, who had done what with whom, and who wanted to do what with whom. It was all just so . . . so not Sara. At least, it never had been before.

Jamie got a really bad, sinking feeling in the pit of her stomach. Over the past summer Kate and Lisa had become, in Jamie's humble opinion, totally guy obsessed. They were so busy thinking about guys that they didn't have time for *American Grrls*.

Jamie had counted on Sara not to join in with their obsession. That would just feel too lonely. Too scary. There was more to the world than just guys.

Now she wondered if maybe she couldn't count on Sara anymore.

Chapter

2

As soon as Jamie and Sara set foot again in Jamie's bedroom, Kate stood up and started chanting, "Food! Must have junk food!" She walked toward them, her arms out straight like those of Frankenstein's monster.

Jamie set the popcorn and cookies down. "Eat, monster."

Kate snatched a cookie and gobbled it down in three bites. Then she grabbed another and sat down next to the food. "Okay, who wants to be the asker first?" She looked at all of them, still chewing her cookie. No one volunteered.

"I will, then," Kate decided, licking chocolate off her pinkie. She turned to Lisa. "Lees, you have to say who's hotter: Scott Carville or Danny Bricktor."

"Gee, tough one," Lisa said, giggling, because Scott was a very cute guy in their class and everyone knew Lisa liked him—including Scott. As for Danny, he was the shortest guy in their entire grade, and he looked like he was about twelve. A young twelve.

"I'll have to go with . . . Scott," Lisa decided. "But it wasn't an easy decision." There were smiles and nods all around, of course. In Choose or Lose, if, when it was your turn, you didn't pick the answer that the majority of the others chose for you, you lost the game.

Not that anything happened if you lost, really. The only thing you could lose was your pride.

"See?" Kate nudged one fuzzy-slippered foot into Jamie's left leg. "That wasn't so mean."

You might not agree with that if you were Danny Bricktor, Jamie thought. But she didn't say anything out loud.

Kate stretched her sinewy arms over her head and eyed Sara. "Sara, Sara, Sara . . . I need the perfect question to ask Sara. . . .

"Got it! Okay. Who would you rather be stuck with on a desert island? Mr. Hathaway or Mr. Benton?"

"Euww," Lisa muttered. "That is an incredibly nasty thought."

Sara bit her lower lip thoughtfully, and Jamie could see she was having trouble making up her mind. Mr. Hathaway, the swim coach, was young, muscular, and really good-looking, but everyone knew he wasn't exactly the brightest star in the firmament. As for Mr. Benton, he'd been teaching biology at LaGrange High School for so long that he'd taught many of their parents. And three weeks ago, when they were dissecting a frog, his false teeth had actually fallen into a shallow dish of frog-soaked formaldehyde.

Everyone knew Benton was brilliant, though. And in amazing physical shape. Even at whatever advanced age he was, he still led wilderness survival treks in Arkansas during summer vacation.

"Can I choose someone else? Like, uh, none of the above?" Sara asked hopefully.

Kate shook her head. "Nope."

"Well, then, I'd have to say . . . Mr. Benton," Sara replied. "Because at least then I'd have a shot at getting off the island."

"Judges?" Kate asked.

Kate and Lisa said "Hathaway" at the same time that Jamie said "Benton."

"Benton?" Lisa marveled. "You guys would really rather be stuck on a desert island with Benton?" She shuddered at the thought. "Besides, look at it this way. If you were with Hathaway, why would you want to get off the island?"

That cracked them all up. Even Jamie.

"All right, you lost that round, so you get another question," Kate told Sara. "Let's see . . . who would you rather go to the school dance with next Saturday, Marc Larson or Jason Kennedy?"

Sara reddened beneath her golden skin. "You guys, please don't ask me that one."

"Have to answer, them's the rules," Kate sang out gleefully.

Jamie was baffled. *What's Sara so embarrassed about?* Marc and Jason were both okay guys in their class. It wasn't like Sara had ever said much to either of them, except maybe, "No, you can't copy my homework."

"Gotta pick," Lisa reminded Sara. "Let's get a move on here."

"Okay." Sara scrunched her eyes up tight. "I pick . . . Jason."

"I knew it, I knew it, I told you!" Lisa crowed triumphantly.

"You guys—" Sara pleaded, nervously twirling a piece of hair in her fingers.

"I told you she was into him," Lisa told Kate. "It was so obvious."

Obvious, since when? Jamie wondered. She racked her brain to see if she had overlooked some clue about Sara liking Jason. *Something that had happened in English class, maybe? They both liked—*

No. Sara had never said anything to her, and Jamie was supposed to be Sara's best friend. They told each other absolutely everything.

"You guys, you have to promise you won't tell him," Sara begged. "Please."

Kate pretended she was holding a phone. "Uh, hi, Jason? This is Kate. What's up? Listen, did you know that Sara Torres wants to bear your children? As soon as possible? As many as possible?"

Sara gasped theatrically and threw a pillow at Kate, which landed in the popcorn bowl, knocking it over. Kate and Lisa convulsed with laughter.

"Look, you know we wouldn't tell him, Sara," Lisa assured her. She and the others began to scoop up the spilled popcorn. "We're only teasing you."

"Are you sure?" Sara asked.

"Sara, please. This is *us* you're talking to," Kate reminded her, examining some popcorn she'd just picked out of the rug. "You think this popcorn has too much lint on it for me to eat?"

"Gross," Lisa pronounced. Kate tossed the handful of linty popcorn at her.

"Joke, Lees, it was a joke. J-O-K-E. How can anyone who draws such funny cartoons lack a sense of humor? Listen, Sara—if you can't trust your best friends, who can you trust?"

"Yeah, you're right," Sara agreed softly. "I do trust you all. Really." She retrieved the pillow and hugged it.

"So . . . do you think there's any chance that he'll ask me to the dance?" Sara continued.

"I could ask Alan to ask Jason if he likes you," Lisa offered.

"But you and Alan broke up," Sara said. "Two weeks ago. Remember?"

"Well, yeah," Lisa agreed. "But we both decided we wanted to stay friends and everything. Anyway,

Alan and Jason are both on the swim team, and I know they party together, so—?"

Jamie let a small smile curl her lips. This ought to be good. Because even if Sara did like Jason, no way would Sara go for something as juvenile as getting Lisa to ask Alan to ask Jason.

That is so very lame, Jamie thought. *So—so Sweet Valley.*

"Okay," Sara said so softly that Jamie wasn't really sure she had heard her friend say it. "Go ahead. Ask him to ask Jason for me."

"Okay?" Jamie echoed incredulously.

Sara didn't seem to notice. She rushed on. "But, Lees, you can't tell Alan that I asked."

"I won't," Lisa assured her.

"Promise?"

"Promise."

Sara looked over at Jamie, who was so surprised at Sara's behavior that her mouth was hanging open. "What?" Sara asked Jamie. "You think it's a bad idea?"

"I have no idea," Jamie managed. "It's, uh, something you have to decide." She didn't want to put Sara on the spot.

Besides, Jamie thought, *I seem to be the only one of the four of us who thinks Lisa's idea is the lamest thing since his-and-hers butt tattoos.*

"Okay, Jamie's turn," Kate said and grinned.

"Can't wait," Jamie said sarcastically.

Jamie watched Kate's eyes meet Lisa's. Then they both smiled. Like they knew something about Jamie they weren't supposed to know. Jamie got a very odd feeling in the pit of her stomach as Kate turned to her.

"So, Jam," Kate began. "If you were going to go parking out at LaGrange Bayou, who would you rather go with? Joshua Jackson . . ."

Jamie laughed. Her friends knew she thought the guy who played Pacey on *Dawson's Creek* was really cute. Maybe this wasn't going to be embarrassing after all.

"Joshua Jackson," Kate repeated, "or . . . Nick Brooks?"

Nick Brooks. Kate had just said Nick Brooks. Jamie couldn't believe it. There was only one guy she liked— had ever liked—since eighth grade. That was Nick Brooks.

She'd never told Kate. Or Lisa. And she knew she hadn't betrayed her feelings for Nick, either. Everyone said she had the perfect poker face, that she was a person who could hide anything from anyone.

Someone else she knew couldn't do that. And that someone was the only person who knew about Jamie's secret crush on Nick Brooks—her best friend, Sara.

But she'd sworn Sara to secrecy, and Sara would never, ever betray . . .

Jamie turned to her best friend, whose every emotion registered in her eyes. Now Jamie's eyes met Sara's. And held them, until Sara looked away.

Which was how Jamie knew the truth: Sara *had* betrayed her.

Chapter

3

Two nights later—Monday night—Jamie closed her biology book and rubbed her tired eyes. She'd been studying since just after dinner, and it was now nine-thirty. Benton was going to give them a quiz the next day.

I'm ready, Jamie decided. *Even if Benton drops his false teeth right on top of my quiz while I'm answering the first question.*

Through the door to her room, she heard her older sister, Cerise, a psychology major at Tulane, singing along to one of the alternative chick musicians she loved.

Cerise's always had a million boyfriends. As far back as I can remember.

Jamie got up and studied her reflection in the mirror over her dresser. *If I was a guy who didn't know me, would I think I'm cute?* she wondered. Then she smiled in what she hoped was a sexy way, as if she were smiling at a guy.

"You look like an idiot," she told her reflection. "Get a grip."

She threw herself onto her bed and stared up at the ceiling. The worst thing was that even if she could smile at a cute guy the way Kate or Lisa could, she would still not be able to say one single interesting thing after the smile.

My grade in flirting is F. Is the real reason that Kate and Lisa and now even Sara care so much about boys that they know how to talk to them, while I'm totally clueless?

It was funny, in an ironic way. Sometimes she'd chat with guys online, who would send her messages about how cool *American Grrls* was, and then she didn't feel shy or tongue-tied at all. She was witty. She was cute. She was . . . well, everything she wasn't in person.

She got up and pulled her ancient gray sweatshirt on over her T-shirt, then headed down the hall of their ranch house toward the family room, where the computer was. Her parents were really strict about when and how she could go online—stricter than any of her friends' parents. They had let Jamie and her friends create a website for their 'zine. But they controlled Jamie's access code, which meant Jamie could only get on the Internet if they were home.

In three years, Jamie thought to herself, *I'll be away at college. I won't live at home and commute like Cerise does. I'll be able to do whatever I want, whenever I want. And maybe by then I'll have gone out on an actual date with a guy. A guy I like. Who really likes me back.*

Maybe Nick and I will both go to LSU or Tulane or maybe someplace cool and far away like Boston University. Then he'll realize that I'm the perfect girl for him and how funny it is that he never noticed before, and—

Yeah, right. First I'd better figure out how to speak a complete sentence to him.

She padded past Cerise's room—a shrine to Tori Amos, Ani DiFranco, and Jewel—and down to the family room. Her dad was sitting on the couch reading something called *Reviving Ophelia.*

"Can you log me on, Dad?"

"Sure, sweetie. You should check out this book I'm reading. It's great—all about how our culture teaches girls to be passive and how girls lose all their dreams when they reach adolescence."

"Uh-huh."

Her father was always reading books on sociology and psychology, especially those that had anything to do with raising what he called "healthy, self-actualized daughters."

Like he's got a clue about what it's really like to be a teen girl today, Jamie thought. *He's not going to find that in any book.*

Her dad typed in her password, and quickly she was on America Online, under her screen name: 15Jamiesworld. Instantly her buddy list popped up, and guys' screen names filled it.

Richierich. Rich Richardson was a fifteen-year-old second cousin who lived in California.

14ZZZDreamer. Matt Williamson. Matt was a guy who had logged onto her website, read her 'zine, and instantly become a fan. He lived in LaCrosse, Wisconsin, a place Jamie had never heard of and had to find on a map.

ShyGuy. ALTBOY. MrJock. Lots of other names, too. Online, Jamie was an incredibly popular girl.

The first instant message popped up on her screen. From Matt.

14ZZZDreamer: Hey Jamie, how's life?

15Jamiesworld: Cool! How's life in the shadow of the world's biggest six-pack?

144ZZZDreamer: You remember that?

15Jamiesworld: How could I ever forget? It's not every day you have a friend who lives under that much beer.

14ZZZDreamer: Hey, remember, my dad works for that brewery. That beer is gonna send me to college someday.

15Jamiesworld: Yeah, and if you don't get in, you can pitch a tent on top of it.

14ZZZDreamer: LOL

24

Jamie had looked LaCrosse up in a travel book about Wisconsin. In LaCrosse, near one of the breweries that Wisconsin was famous for, there was a series of water tanks that had been painted to look like cans of beer from that brewery. The whole thing was billed as the world's largest six-pack, and it was a minor tourist attraction.

14ZZZDreamer: So what else is going on?

15Jamiesworld: Not much. School dance on Saturday. Why aren't you here to take me?

14ZZZDreamer: Believe me, I wish I was taking you. So, what lucky guy is it gonna be?

15Jamiesworld: Oh, Matt, there are just soooo many. I can hardly make up my mind.

14ZZZDreamer: :(I bet they're lining up. They should be lining up. Wish I was there. By the way, nice review of MTV's "Rock the Vote" concert on your website. I thought Courtney Love was annoying, too.

15Jamiesworld: Yeah, yeah. But it's not the whole 'zine. I miss the whole 'zine. Maybe you should consider changing sexes and moving here to help me.

Jamie smiled. Matt was such a nice guy. He was so easy to talk to on the computer. Funny. Nice. And always himself. Cute, too. They'd exchanged pictures. He wasn't Nick, of course. But then, who could be?

And Matt likes me. He thinks I'm funny. And cute.

And a great writer. So why can I talk to him online when I know that in person, or even on the phone, I'd be a total disaster?

In the kitchen the phone rang, and Jamie heard her mother answer it. A moment later her mom popped her head into the family room. "Jam? It's for you. Sara."

Sara. Ever since Saturday, things hadn't felt right with Sara, but Jamie hadn't come right out and asked her if she'd told Kate and Lisa about Nick. It seemed so obvious that she had.

"Tell her I'll be right there."

Jamie typed a quick goodbye to Matt, because her parents insisted that when she was on the phone or the computer, the other incoming line had to be free. Then she picked up the portable phone and took it over to the couch, which her father had so conveniently vacated.

"Hey, Sara."

Her friend let out a wild whoop of joy that made Jamie's eardrums rattle.

Chapter

4

"*W*ow, what's that about?" Jamie asked, once her ear recovered the ability to hear.

"Just the greatest thing in the world."

"Angela came home?" Angela was the sister who had dropped out of high school. The last anyone knew, she was in Florida with some guy. Sara's family worried about her all the time.

"Better than that," Sara said breathily. "Much better."

"What could be better?"

"Jason."

"Jason Kennedy? Jason Kennedy is better than Angela coming home?" Jamie was slightly aghast at her friend's sense of priorities.

"Yes! Remember what we were talking about

with Kate and Lisa Saturday night? Well, Lisa asked Alan to ask Jason whether he liked me and Jason told Alan yes and Alan told Lisa and Lisa called me and then Jason called me and ever since then we've—"

"Whoa, time out, take time to inhale," Jamie interrupted her friend.

"Sorry, it's just that I'm so excited I can hardly stand it."

"So, what happened, exactly?" Jamie asked, bemused.

"Okay, this is it. Jason called me at seven o'clock and now it's nine-thirty and we've been on the phone for two and a half hours. *Hours.* He is so incredible."

"Your parents let you stay on the phone for two and a half hours?" Jamie asked.

"They just got home, so they don't know about it," Sara confided, her voice dropping low. "Oh, my gosh, Jamie, Jason is just so . . . he's so great."

"Well, I'm really happy for you," Jamie said, trying to muster some enthusiasm.

"You don't sound happy."

"I am, Sara. Of course I am."

But was she, really? Jamie wasn't sure what she was feeling. A lot of things, really. Yes, Sara was her best friend, so she was truly happy for her that the guy she liked liked her back. And, yes, Jason seemed like a pretty good guy.

But the whole thing of getting Alan to ask Jason was

so lame, Jamie thought. *And Sara never blows off her homework to talk on the phone on a school night. Not a good sign.*

"Did you study for Benton's quiz?" she asked Sara.

"I can't think about that now," Sara said. "I'll have to study late tonight. Or get up early. Or something."

Wow. It was even worse than Jamie had thought. Sara sounded like she'd been taken over by the pod people or something.

She's gonna flunk Benton's quiz, and her parentals will ground her. And—

You're jealous, a little voice in the back of her head taunted. *You're jealous because she can be herself with the guy she likes, and he likes her back. You're just jealous. She'd be happy for you if Nick Brooks had called you.*

"Jam? Are you there?"

"I'm here. Listen, Sara, I am really, really happy for you."

"Really?"

"Really. I just . . . my mind was on Benton's quiz, I guess. Jason seems really cool. And he's lucky to get a girl as cool as you are to like him back."

"Thanks, Jam. You're the best."

"So, did you write that story you were thinking about for the website, about bilingual education in public schools?"

"Huh?" Sara asked.

"Forget it," Jamie sighed. "Tell me, did Jason ask you to the dance?"

Jamie held her breath. She and Sara had planned to go to the school dance together, since neither of them had a date. They'd done it lots of times. But now if Sara was going with Jason . . .

"He didn't, not yet," Sara admitted. "But it was a first phone call. I'm hoping tomorrow."

Jamie exhaled.

"Jam?" Sara went on. "You know, Jason is kind of a friend of Nick's."

"So?"

"Well—" Sara hesitated.

"Yes?"

"Well, you know how Lisa got Alan to talk to Jason, and that's how Jason called me. So if you want—I'm only asking as a friend, so don't get mad—I could ask Jason to ask Nick if he likes you. You know. Really likes you. Like *likes* you."

"No," Jamie blurted out emphatically before she could think about how ungrateful she sounded.

"You don't have to get mad about it—"

"I'm not," Jamie assured Sara. "It's just—look, I'm sorry, Sara, but isn't that ask-a-guy-to-ask-his-bud stuff kind of like a middle-school thing?"

"You think I'm acting like I'm in sixth grade?"

"No, no, forget it," Jamie said quickly. "I didn't mean that the way it came out."

At the other end of the phone, Sara was silent.

"Sar? You mad?"

"No."

"You sure?"

"I'm sure. But I wish you'd think about it, Jam. I mean, I know you like Nick. There's nothing embarrassing about that. I'm sure he'd like you, too, if he only knew that you—"

"I can't," Jamie interrupted. "I just can't."

"Well, if you change your mind, let me know."

The thought made Jamie's skin crawl.

"I could even help you figure out stuff to say to him—I know how shy you get around guys, Jamie," Sara went on. "And then they don't ever really get the chance to get to know the real you."

"Something about it just . . . thanks anyway, Sara."

"Okay," Sara said. "But if you change your mind, you can always call—"

Click-click, as Sara's call-waiting clicked in. "Hold on a sec," Sara instructed, and the line went quiet as Sara shifted to the other call. Ten seconds later she was back.

"Jam? Oh, my gosh, it's him! I have to go."

"Him?"

"Jason. He's calling me again!" Sara exclaimed happily. "Maybe to ask me to the dance. I'll tell you tomorrow in school. Bye!"

The line went dead in Jamie's hands.

Wow.

It was as if her best friend Sara, the smartest girl

in the entire tenth grade, had just experienced a brain drain of about fifty IQ points. *She hung up on me in the middle of a conversation*, Jamie thought, *so she could talk to him.*

Jamie wandered back to her room, a million conflicting thoughts pulling on her at once. Like how awful it felt to be pushed aside by her best friend, just because a guy called. *But on the other hand . . .*

What would it be like to talk on the phone to the guy I really like for hours and hours—twice in one night?

"Like I'll find out in this lifetime," she said aloud.

She threw herself on her bed and closed her eyes, the better to daydream about Nick and her, together at the dance.

An hour later she was getting ready to get into bed when she decided the room felt stuffy. *I'll open a window*, she decided. *It's cool out, but not so much that I'll get cold.*

She padded over to the big window on the opposite side of her room, unlocked it, and opened it. The window faced the backyard, where Jamie's dad kept his big vegetable garden and her mother the hammock that she liked to take naps in in the summertime. It was a glorious autumn night, and Jamie inhaled deep lungfuls of cool air. It felt wonderful to be alive.

Later, when she thought about it, she couldn't figure out what made her look straight down at the ground, under her window. But she did. And that's when she saw it, glinting in the moonlight, stuck in the lower branches of a shrub with stickers.

What is that?

Jamie took a closer look at the object lying in the bright wash of the backyard security floodlights. It appeared to be made of glass, but not any kind of glass she'd ever seen before. It was about the size of a softball. And it was positively gleaming.

But it was buried in the shrubbery. Impossible to reach in for without getting totally scratched.

How then to get it out? Jamie had an overwhelming desire to get her hands on the object. *I know!*

Quickly she ran out of her room, down to a storage closet where her father kept all his sporting equipment. She rummaged through it, pushing tennis rackets and fishing rods aside, looking for—

There it is! In the back!

Hung on a hook, at the back of the closet, was the long-handled dip net that her father used to pluck minnows and small fish out of the shallows of the bayous to use as bait. Jamie grabbed the net, turned to go back to her room—

And practically smacked into her father.

"Taking up fishing, Jamie?" her father asked wryly.

"Uh, not exactly, but—"

"Because I'd love to take you out sometime. What a great father-daughter activity!"

"But—"

"Think about it," her dad counseled.

"I need to measure the netting for a geometry project for school," Jamie invented.

Her dad nodded, actually a little disappointed. "Just make sure it gets back in the closet. And if you ever want to go fishing—"

"Will do. G'night, Daddy," Jamie said.

"G'night, sweetie."

Carrying the dip net, Jamie walked back to her room and then straight to her open window. Thirty seconds later the rock—or whatever it was—was safely in the dip net, on the floor of Jamie's room.

She reached down and plucked it up, marveling at how beautiful it was. The thing was the color of pink roses in the summer—no, the first pink roses of late spring. When Jamie turned it over, she saw it had matching, glassy, oval-shaped sides that slanted first outward and then in to a single point. It looked like a valentine from outer space.

It's lovely, she thought. *Where did it come from? And what is it?*

The more she looked at it, the more she was convinced that it was some kind of a love offering. And as she held it, she got the warmest feeling inside.

Well, she thought as she placed the object on her nightstand so that she could look at it after she got into bed. *This has been an interesting evening.*

Then something strange happened. Jamie felt compelled to pick it up again. She did. The rock *vibrated,* almost as if it had a power source within it that made it shake.

The sensation made Jamie laugh. It tickled her palm more than anything else. *I'm losing my mind,* she thought. *Laughing at a rock because it's tickling my hand?*

"No. Not a rock. A Loverock."

"Who said that?" Jamie asked out loud. The voice that said "No. Not a rock. A Loverock" was as clear as Sara's had been on the phone.

I am definitely losing it, Jamie thought, quickly placing the Loverock on her nightstand. *And if I wake up and the Loverock has turned into a handsome prince, then I will know it's time to check myself into the nearest psychiatric hospital.*

Chapter

5

"No, he was an alien all along," Jamie insisted. "Didn't you get that?" She was sitting with Sara and Lisa at their usual table in the cafeteria, talking about the previous night's episode of *Roswell High*.

"You guys, I have something huge to tell you," Kate said, rushing over to join them. She had the biggest grin on her face.

"Tell us what?" Lisa asked.

Kate pulled a chair up next to Jamie's and plucked up one of Jamie's French fries, popping it daintily into her mouth. "Mmm. Dee-lish."

"Hey," Jamie said. "If you want a French fry, take about ten at once, okay?"

Her friends all laughed, and she did, too. They always stole food from one another's plates. "So, what's the big excitement?" Sara asked.

"The big excitement is one more round of Choose or Lose," Kate announced. "Right now, like it or not."

Everyone groaned, Jamie the loudest. "Again?" she asked. "And now? Aren't you ready for a different game? How about Chutes and Ladders? Or maybe Candyland? Something really tough. And— you know—mind-expanding."

"Oh, go ahead and joke, but I think you're gonna want to play this round, Jam." Kate's voice dropped confidentially. "Trust me on this one."

"Go ahead, Jamie," Sara encouraged her. "If she gets out of line, we'll spill our Cokes on her."

"Choose or Lose," Kate repeated. "With Jamie. Right now."

Jamie sighed. "Okay, okay, Choose or Lose. What's the question?"

Kate grinned conspiratorially. "The question? What makes you think there's a question? No. No question."

"Is this conversation supposed to make sense?" Jamie asked.

Kate smiled, shaking her hair off her face. "I'm changing the rules. Because I have the answer. In fact, the definitive answer. But only if Jamie asks the definitive question."

"All righty, then," Jamie said. "The question is,

has former 'zine writer but now overly hormonally influenced Kate McGee lost her mind, or has she only apparently lost her mind?"

"Not amusing," Kate replied. Then she leaned in to the group, her eyes sparkling. "But just because I'm such a wonderful friend, I'm going to relent and ask the question for you."

Jamie folded her arms. "Well?"

"The question is, Jamie, the same one I asked you on Saturday night at your house. If you were going parking out at LaGrange Bayou, which of the following guys would you want to go with you: Joshua Jackson or Nick Brooks?"

"I take back what I said about hormonal imbalance. Actually, this is what a junk-food overdose can do to the brain," Jamie said, shaking her head ruefully. "It isn't pretty. Isn't there a twelve-step program or something you can start?"

"You're not joking your way out of this, Jamie. Josh or Nick?" Kate repeated.

"Hey," Lisa protested, "no fair. Jamie doesn't even know Josh—"

"Bingo!" Kate chortled. "Ten thousand points for Lisa Sherwin, and may you raise your grades to a B average. Jamie doesn't know Josh Jackson. Josh Jackson doesn't know Jamie. Which leaves us Nick Brooks . . ."

Jamie froze. She'd just figured out what was going on with this game of Choose or Lose.

Oh, no. She asked Nick if he likes me, Jamie thought. *I will never, ever live this down.*

"And the correct answer is . . . Nick Brooks!" Kate exclaimed.

"What does that mean?" Jamie asked slowly.

"That means he likes you," Lisa filled in. "That's what it has to mean."

"No, no, don't thank me, I am but a go-between in the great love story of life," Kate said dramatically. "Oh, yeah, by the way, Nick says he will be glad to see you at the dance on Saturday."

Jamie grabbed Kate's arm, unable to control herself. "Wait a sec. You're telling me that Nick Brooks likes me? *Likes*-me likes me?"

"That is so fantastic," Lisa gushed. "Nick is incredibly cute. You are so lucky, Jamie."

Jamie blushed. She felt just so . . . so weird. Never in a million years would she have wanted Kate to talk to Nick about her. Why, she'd just told Sara the other night that Sara shouldn't even consider getting someone to find out how Nick—

Uh-oh. Sara. She betrayed me once, she'll betray me again—

Jamie looked Sara in the eye, but this time Sara didn't look away.

"Oh, you think Sara told me," Kate realized. "Nopers. Not a chance."

"When it comes to the girl-guy thing," Lisa added, "Kate has radar."

"Thank you," Jamie mouthed to her best friend.

"You're welcome," Sara mouthed back.

"No, you should be thanking me, Jamie," Kate went on in a teasing voice. "But that's okay. I realize you're in a state of shock."

Lisa grabbed Jamie's hands. "Is this cool or what?"

"I—I don't really know," Jamie confessed.

"You will," Kate predicted. "Now, the final question—to the girl who puts down guy-obsessed girls but who, under it all, is completely Nick-ified, so to speak—is now that you know, what are you going to do about it?"

What Jamie did about it for the rest of the week was—nothing. In fact, she did her very best to pretend the whole conversation with her friends had never happened. She went about her life at school as she always did. She got an A on the biology quiz from Benton, and was sympathetic to Sara when Sara only made a B minus. She worked in the public library on Tuesdays and Thursdays after school.

She called Sara to try to get her to post a story on their website about the latest scandal in their school. A teacher had been accused of giving the same tests to her history students year after year after year.

No luck. All Sara wanted to talk about was Jason Kennedy.

Jamie went online when she finished her homework, posted a scathing review of the new Limp Bizkit album on their 'zine website—feeling sick that the actual 'zine hadn't come out in so long—and chatted with Matt for a while.

Before she went to bed, she looked at her Loverock for a long time every night. When she picked it up, sometimes, she felt it vibrate, but at other times she was sure it was her imagination. But about Nick? Nothing. Even when her friends asked her about him—and they did, all the time—she changed the subject.

"You better get a clue, Jamie," Kate had finally said to her on Friday. "If a guy likes a girl and he gets absolutely no sign from her that she likes him back, he's gonna move on."

Move on? How could Nick move on from something that had never happened? Jamie knew she'd be lying if she said she wasn't thinking about Nick at all. Or noticing things about him. Like, that he seemed to spend an awful lot of time looking at her. In the cafeteria. In English class. At her locker. But he didn't say anything to her.

If he likes me so much, Jamie wondered, *why doesn't he ever say two words to me?*

Now it was Saturday night, and she and Sara were getting dressed for the school dance. And Jamie still didn't know the answer to that question.

Unless . . .

"Do you think that maybe Nick Brooks is shy?" Jamie asked Sara.

Sara stood in front of Jamie's mirror and turned her head this way and that, playing with her hair. "Do you think Jason will like it better down or up?"

"Whatever," Jamie replied. "Did you hear my question?"

Sara let her hair fall to her shoulders. "I heard you. And you don't have to be mean. I just wanted your opinion."

"I'm sorry," Jamie said quickly. "Really. And your hair looks wonderful up. Regal. He'll love that."

Sara lifted her hair again and studied the effect. "Really?"

"Really. Now, can you answer my question?"

Sara went and sat next to Jamie on her bed. "Well, have you said anything to him?"

Jamie fiddled with her charm bracelet. "No. Not really."

"Then maybe it's like Kate said," Sara mused. "You know. That he doesn't know you like him and he doesn't want to make a fool of himself if you don't."

"But how could he make a fool of himself just by talking to me?" Jamie asked, frustrated.

"According to my older brothers and sisters, guys can be just as crazy as girls about these things," Sara said, shrugging. She began to twist her hair up into a messy knot, securing it with hairpins. "What does Cerise say about this stuff?"

Jamie shrugged. "I never ask, she never tells."

"See, from his point of view," Sara continued, "Nick has already made the first move, by telling Kate that he likes you." She sprayed her hair with silver glitter hair spray. "Which means that according to him, the ball's in your court."

"Why does it have to be a ball, and why does it have to be in my court?" Jamie commented, leaning back on her bed. "This isn't some game."

"Yes, it is. That's the way it is, that's the way it always has been, and that's the way it always will be," Sara pronounced. "Does my hair look okay now?"

Jamie sat up so she could see. "Perfect. Since when do you know so much about guys, anyway?"

Sara shrugged. "I guess it comes from being the youngest in a big family."

Jamie sighed. "I remember seventh grade," she began. "We all used to just hang out, with Kyle Mackey and Mario Angelino and all these other guys. And all the great times we had with the 'zine. There wasn't this whole boyfriend-girlfriend thing all the time. It ruins everything."

Sara came back over to the bed and sat next to Jamie. "Can I tell you something honestly? As your best friend?"

"Of course."

"The problem is not the boyfriend-girlfriend thing. If people didn't ever get to the boyfriend-girlfriend thing, no one would get married, or have children, or anything."

"I suppose."

"And the problem isn't that Nick likes you and you don't like him, because you do," Sara went on in her soft voice.

"And so by process of elimination, the problem is?" Jamie asked.

"The problem is," Sara pronounced, "that you, Jamie Dobrin, are scared to death of talking to Nick. Because you like him so much."

"True," Jamie admitted.

"And when you like a guy, you turn into Robogirl around him. I've seen it happen before."

"No, I don't."

Sara gave her a knowing look.

"Okay, maybe I do." Jamie fussed with the hem of her skirt. "But what am I supposed to do about it?"

Sara wagged a finger at her. "Tonight is your absolutely golden opportunity. It's a dance. Where the operative word is *dance*. Not have-a-deep-discussion-with-a-select-member-of-the-opposite-sex-about-the-future-of-the-universe-and-whether-the-Big-Bang-theory-is-really-true. A *dance*."

Jamie laughed in spite of herself. "But what if—what if he asks me to dance and my mind just goes blank and—"

Sara made a swift move toward the boom box on Jamie's dresser and turned it on; a Rage Against the Machine tape started to play. She turned to

Jamie and scrunched up her shoulders, doing her best imitation of a guy.

"Hey, Jamie, wazzup, wha's happening?" Her voice was deep and gravelly.

"That doesn't sound anything like Nick!" Jamie said, sputtering with laughter.

Sara refused to laugh with her. She just made her voice even deeper and said, "Hey, wanna dance?"

"I feel like an idiot, Sara—"

"The name's Nick. Wanna dance?"

"Uh, sure . . . Nick." Jamie got to her feet. "I'd love to."

Sara pushed the Off button on the boom box. "See? No problem. It was easy."

"At the risk of pointing out the obvious, you're Sara, not Nick."

"Use your very vivid imagination," Sara suggested. She looked down at Jamie's outfit and frowned. "And while you're at it, why don't you change into that new skirt you got at the mall last week?"

"I was thinking of returning it," Jamie explained. "It's kind of short, don't you think?"

"I think it's kind of perfect," Sara told her.

Jamie quickly pulled off her old skirt and put on the new one. She looked in the mirror. It looked so red.

And so short.

"Fantastic," Sara assured her. "Now fix your hair and everything. We've only got two hours."

"It doesn't take two hours to get ready," Jamie grumbled.

Sara smiled mischievously. "Of course it doesn't. Fifteen more minutes to get dressed. And one hour and forty-five minutes to practice saying, 'Yes, Nick, I'd love to dance!' "

Chapter

6

*J*amie stared nervously at her reflection in the mirror above the sinks in the school bathroom. She and her three best friends had gone from Kate's car directly into the bathroom. Jamie had begged them to.

I look like I'm trying too hard, Jamie thought glumly. A red rhinestone barrette held back part of her dark brown hair. It matched her skirt.

Her really, really short skirt.

"You guys, are you sure this skirt isn't too—"

"We may have to put her out of our misery," Kate joked to the others. "Jamie, listen to me. You look hot. Really hot. Hot is good."

"Hot is good," Jamie echoed, as if saying it out loud would help her to convince herself.

"Hey, can we get in there before the guys we like start liking someone else?" Lisa asked.

"What is this, middle school?" Jamie began. "If they're that fickle, then—"

Her friends wouldn't let her finish her sentence. Instead they edged her out of the bathroom to face the music. And Nick.

The school gym had been turned into the Four Seasons, the theme of the dance. There were murals on the walls of scenes from winter, fall, summer, and spring, and appropriate refreshments for each season. The "autumn" table held apple cider and doughnuts, for example, and there was even a mountain of dried leaves and hay in the corner. Of course, guys were already jumping into the pile and getting hay everywhere.

Nearby, the DJ they'd hired was spinning tunes and twirling a piece of hay in his mouth. A hip-hop song with a huge back beat was blasting out of the speakers.

"Have fun, you guys," Kate called out as she immediately headed over to Ben Rogers, the guy she'd recently started seeing.

"How does she do that?" Jamie wondered. "Until three weeks ago, it was Dougie, Dougie, Dougie. Now it's Ben, Ben, Ben. Doesn't she get dizzy?"

"Self-confidence," Sara replied. "When you stop and think about it, she's been like that since we've known her."

"She's getting worse," Jamie said darkly.

"Hey, Lees, what's up?" Scott Carville said, strolling over to them.

"Not much," Lisa replied casually. Jamie was hanging on every word, but pretending not to. Because maybe she could just copy whatever it was Lisa said to Scott.

So far, so good.

"So, did you hear about Mike Bozell?" Scott asked.

"No, what?"

"He got caught drinking a brew outside just now. Mr. Hathaway turned him over to the rent-a-cops."

"Wow, is he gonna get suspended?" Lisa asked. " 'Cause last year, when he—"

Scott shrugged. "You know what a fool Bozell is. Like, how brain dead do you have to be to bring beer to a school dance? Answer: very."

Lisa giggled. "No kidding. Maybe he should have invited us and his buds over to his house to drink it." Jamie blanched, but no one noticed.

Scott laughed. "So, wanna dance?"

"Sure," Lisa said.

Scott reached out, and Lisa took his hand. "Later," she told Jamie and Sara over her shoulder as she headed out to dance with Scott.

Jamie turned to Sara. "Okay, what *was* that?"

"What was what?"

"Lisa just made this unbelievably insipid comment about going drinking over at Mike's house. Lisa doesn't drink!"

Sara shrugged. "She was just making conversation. Oh, look, there's Jason," Sara whispered, squeezing Jamie's hand tight. "He looks cute in a jacket, don't you think?"

"Uh-huh."

Jamie hardly noticed Jason. Because her stomach was churning like a commercial for antacid. Her head was pounding, not because she had seen Nick, but because she knew she was too afraid even to look around to see if Nick was there.

"Jason's coming over here."

"Calm down. He's not Ricky Martin," Jamie muttered as Jason stepped over to them.

"Hi, Sara," Jason said, grinning. "Hey, Jamie."

"Hi," Jamie said.

"Wow, you look fantastic, Sara. Your hair is amazing."

"Thanks!"

Jamie slid her eyes over to Sara, who was glowing as if she were radioactive.

"Check out that hay thing," Jason said, cocking his head toward the other side of the gym. "It's all over the place already. Every time someone jumps into it, the hay flies onto the DJ's turntables. It's a riot."

"Who was on the decoration committee?" Sara asked, laughing. "I have a feeling whoever dreamed up the haystack will never volunteer again."

"Tell me about it," Jason agreed. "So, you want to dance?"

Sara hesitated, turning to Jamie. "It's fine," Jamie assured her. "Go."

Sara shook her head. "I'm not leaving you here by yourself."

"I'm not exactly a one-girl pity party, okay?" Jamie said, her voice low. "Go dance. Now. You know you—"

Someone tugged on a lock of Jamie's hair. She turned around.

Nick.

"Hey," he said, smiling at her, as Jason and Sara headed off to the dance floor.

"Hey."

"Bye," Sara called back to them. She was alone. With Nick.

Not alone, exactly, Jamie amended in her mind. *At a dance. With tons of people. People you know. It's not like you have to worry that Nick is going to grab you and kiss you and—*

"Something wrong?" Nick asked.

"Huh?"

"Your face just got all red."

"Oh."

Nick stuck his hands into his pockets. "I just wondered. Maybe cuz it's hot in here."

"It is?" Jamie asked. Then she winced. What an incredibly dumb thing to say. *I mean, she had her own nerve endings. She could tell that it was hot.*

Nick shrugged. He looked everywhere except at her. So she looked everywhere except at him.

Acid churned in her stomach. *Say something, say something, say something,* she commanded her mind. *Something cute. Something funny and flirtatious. Something like, "Are we really supposed to believe it's autumn in New England when it was eighty-something degrees out today?"*

Yes. That would be perfect. She opened her mouth to say it.

Out came the most humongous belch.

"Oh, God, excuse me, I'm so . . ." Jamie's hand flew to her mouth. "My stomach's a little . . ."

"S'no biggie," Nick mumbled, staring down at his feet as if his left shoe had just gotten really interesting.

"Sorry," Jamie mumbled again.

"You want some cider?" Nick asked, still displaying great interest in his shoes. "Maybe it'll settle your stomach."

"Okay."

"I'll go get you some. There was a whole keg of it when the dance started." He took off toward the long table that held the refreshments.

When Jamie saw that he was halfway to the refreshments area, she ran out of the gym and sagged against the wall in the hallway.

Oh, God. She just let out a huge belch in front of the first guy she had ever liked. She had embarrassed herself forever. What were her friends going to think when it got around?

It's like one of those agony moments from Seventeen *magazine,* she thought. *Only it's not funny.*

Kate came hurrying down the hall, back from the water fountain. She had almost passed Jamie when she saw her friend. "Jamie! What're you doing out here?"

Jamie told Kate what had happened.

"Oh, wow, that is super embarrassing," Kate sympathized. "What a drag."

Jamie nodded miserably. "He asked if I wanted some cider just so he'd have an excuse to get away from me."

"Maybe not, maybe he really went—"

"Maybe not?" Jamie echoed. "He didn't say, 'I'll be right back.' And he took off so fast you would have thought a hundred and one pit bulls were chasing him."

Kate bit her lower lip thoughtfully. "Okay, there's only one way to deal with this," she decided.

"Crawl into a hole and die?"

"No. Go back in there and act like nothing happened," Kate pronounced.

"But it did happen," Jamie said. "Pretending it didn't happen won't make it not have happened."

"Come on," Kate coaxed her. "I'll go with you."

Jamie sighed, but she let Kate lead her toward the gym. She looked around. "I don't see him."

"I'm sure he's here somewhere," Kate said, scanning the room.

"Maybe I grossed him out so completely that he

went to the bathroom to barf and then went home." The moment of her humiliation played over and over in her mind, especially the look on Nick's face when she'd belched—

"Speaking of going home, what a good idea," Jamie said. "I know you don't want to leave, Kate, so I'll just call my—"

"You're not running away," Kate said firmly. "Now, let's find Nick. And remember, be cool. Like nothing happened. Okay?"

"Can I say yes and mean no?"

Kate groaned. "Come on."

The worked their way through the crowded room, Kate looking for Nick, Jamie looking at the floor.

"Hi, you guys!" Lisa called. "Having fun?"

Jamie looked up. Lisa was dancing with Scott. She looked so pretty and happy and at ease.

"A blast," Kate called back. "Catch ya later."

"Kate, let's just forget it," Jamie suggested.

Kate turned to Jamie, hands on her slender hips. "Look, I'm gonna be straight with you, Jam. I love you. You're terrific. But when you get around guys, you turn into an entirely different person. And if you don't get over it, no decent guy is ever gonna like you."

Tears sprang to Jamie's eyes.

"Oh, Jam, I didn't mean to hurt your feelings, it's just that—"

"No, you didn't. It's okay."

Jamie wasn't looking at Kate. She was looking past her.

"Then what—?"

Kate turned around, to see what had Jamie's attention. The music had turned slow and romantic. The lights were dimmed. There was Nick. Slow dancing. With another girl.

Jamie fled.

"Jam!"

She heard Kate calling her, but she just kept running. Through the crowd. Out of the gym. Outside, where she could deal with her humiliation in private. All the way out into the middle of the football field, where the noise and music of the dance were barely perceptible.

She stared up at the clear night sky.

How can the heavens look so perfect when down on Earth my life is so messed up?

"If only I could be like Kate. Or Lisa. Or even Sara," Jamie whispered to the stars. "They know how to talk to boys. How to flirt and get boys to like them.

"And me—I know how to belch."

She closed her eyes tight and wrapped her arms around herself.

Please, she prayed, *please let me change. Let me learn how to flirt.*

She opened her eyes to the stars once more. "It's not really so much to ask, is it?" she said. "I haven't been able to flirt with guys for fifteen years and five months.

"So now, I'm asking. Could you just give me the flirting gene? So that I can talk to Nick? So that he'll fall in love with me? Please?"

And then she thought: *Funny thing about the stars. Twinkling away up there, they seem to promise everything.*

But they never, ever answer your wish.

Chapter

7

It played over and over in Jamie's mind.

She lay in bed, unable to sleep. The two minutes that she had spent with Nick Brooks in the gym—the two most embarrassing minutes of her life—stuck in her mind like a terrible nightmare, no matter how she kept telling herself that she was overreacting and that everyone burps.

But not in front of a crush, Jamie thought. *Not when a girl's never been able to put two words together in front of him that sound remotely intelligent. When he said it was hot in the gym, there were a million things I could have said.*

I could have said: "Yeah, it sure is hot. We should have made this a pool party theme." Or: "Maybe no one told us and it's supposed to be a sauna in autumn in New England." Or—something. Anything!

Anything except belching in his face.

She sighed. No wonder she and Kate had found him dancing with some other girl. A girl who could actually carry on a conversation. And not belch.

I'm not just one agony column in Seventeen *magazine. I'm good for the whole issue.*

She rolled over again and realized she wasn't going to get to sleep any time soon, which made her think about going downstairs and logging onto AOL to chat with some of her friends. Maybe she would tell them what happened, and they could all laugh about it like the ridiculous thing it was.

But that option was out. Her parents were already in bed and wouldn't let her go online without their being around.

They treat me like I'm twelve instead of fifteen, she thought irritably. Then she frowned. As if getting angry at her parents could make it easier to deal with how angry she was at herself.

She sat up and flicked on the light switch. The first thing she noticed was a magazine on her nightstand, with the cover blurb: "Why Shy Girls Come in Last."

"Oh, that's very helpful." She switched the light off again and lay in the dark to think about all the things she should have said and done differently. Moonlight illuminated the Loverock on her nightstand. It was so beautiful. So timeless. So silent and constant.

"And no one expects it to carry on a scintillating conversation," she said aloud.

Then she laughed. Because that comment was funny. Her real self was funny. Now, if only she could be her real self around guys.

She reached for the Loverock, picked it up, and held it to the moonlight. Once again she had the weird sensation that the Loverock was vibrating in her hands. Suddenly an impetuous thought jumped into her head:

I'm going to sleep with it, Jamie decided. *I know it's stupid, but I'm going to put it under my pillow. When I was little, the tooth fairy would bring me money when I lost a tooth. Maybe the Loverock will . . . bring me the ability to flirt with guys.*

Right.

Okay, so it was stupid. But it couldn't be any stupider than what had happened with Nick.

And at least alone in my bedroom, no one can witness just how stupid I can be.

She quickly stuck it under her pillow as if she were hiding it from someone.

"What am I doing?" she muttered. She had no idea. But she put her head on her pillow, moving around until she found a good position—one where it didn't feel like a rock was jamming into her head.

She closed her eyes. Nick. There he was in her mind's eye. Those great brown eyes and that dimple in his chin when he smiled.

Not that he'd ever smiled at her, exactly. Not that he ever would.

Part of her wished she really were still twelve. Or even fourteen. Everything had been so much simpler then. Just she and her three best friends. They never talked about boyfriends, or who liked whom. They talked about their own lives and what they liked and what they wanted to do. They worked on their 'zine. They were doing something with their lives. Instead of talking about guys, guys, guys. Like guys was the only topic on earth.

No wonder I get tongue-tied around guys, Jamie thought, sighing. *My friends act like guys are the only important thing in life. Even Sara.*

Who can face that kind of pressure?

Still, as she drifted off to dream, she saw herself and Nick, dancing together to Tori Amos. She felt perfect in his arms. She said the right thing and she did the right thing. Nick thought she was the most wonderful, fantastic, darling girl in the universe. In fact, every guy at the dance was staring at them, and thinking that Nick was the luckiest guy at the dance, because he was with her.

It was a wonderful, wonderful dream.

"Jamie!" Sara exclaimed happily, when Jamie came down the front walk Monday morning. "Hi!"

"Sara!" Jamie mimicked Sara's shocked voice. "We walk to school together every morning, so why do you sound so surprised to see me?"

"Well, Kate told me what happened Saturday night," Sara admitted. "And I haven't talked to you since it happened, so—"

"You don't have to refer to the Big Belch Blunder as 'it,' " Jamie said, brushing a strand of hair out of her eyes. "It's not like I committed a major felony."

"I know. And I'm sure it wasn't as bad as Lisa says—" Sara clapped her hand over her mouth, blushing furiously.

"So Lisa knows too?" Jamie demanded. "What, did Kate tell everyone what happened?"

"Well . . . probably not everyone," Sara said, retracting her words meekly. "Just your friends."

"How am I ever going to live this down?"

Sara gave her a quick hug. "I'll tell you the truth, Jamie. It isn't so awful. Even if other people do know, by tomorrow everyone will be gossiping about someone else who did something else."

"I suppose that's true."

"It is," Sara said emphatically. With a twinkle in her eye, she added, "I was afraid you weren't going to come out of your room."

Jamie laughed. "To tell you the truth, I thought about it, but—"

"Hey, how's it going?" a friendly, male voice called from behind them.

They turned around. Drake Frazier was headed toward them, loping the easy long-strided walk of a basketball player, which is exactly what he was. Not to mention a senior. And a highly fine one, at that.

Jamie and Sara were two of only four sophomores in LaGrange High School's only psychology class, and Drake was in their class. He also lived down the street from them. And, as everyone knew, seniors didn't exactly hang out with sophomores.

He usually drives to school, Jamie thought, *even though it's walking distance. So I wonder why——?*

"My car's in the shop," he told them as if he had read Jamie's mind. The three of them started walking together toward school as if it were the most natural thing in the world.

"What's wrong with it?" Jamie asked.

"Overheating," Drake said. "It's gonna cost me a bundle to get it fixed, too. I have a feeling the guy at the service station is taking me for a major ride on the price, but I know zip about cars, so how can I argue?"

"Try Lerner's technique," Jamie suggested, naming their psychology teacher. "When the guy at the service station gives you the bill, just say, 'I think you can do better.' "

Drake laughed, and so did Sara. Ms. Lerner was famous for cowing people into improving their research papers by handing them back their papers and saying: "I think you can do better." It almost always worked, too.

"Maybe I should just send Lerner down to the garage for me," Drake said.

"I would eat the mystery meat in the cafeteria

just to be there when you ask her to do it," Jamie said, chuckling.

"That's almost tempting," Drake said. "No one has eaten that stuff since, like, Nixon was president."

"They should send it to the Smithsonian to study," Jamie said. "You never know what you might find in it. The Missing Link. Bigfoot—"

Drake smiled and cocked his head at her. "You know, you're funny."

"I take it you mean that as a compliment," Jamie replied in a teasing voice.

"I just never noticed, I guess," Drake said.

"Oh, that's because I have multiple personalities," Jamie explained. "See, you're talking to Alberta right now. She's gonna be a stand-up comic. She's a little manic but quite entertaining."

Drake grinned at her. "Nice to meet you, Alberta."

They'd reached the front of the school, and Drake was gazing down at her with frank admiration in his eyes. "I have to say, Jamie/Alberta, you made walking to school almost painless."

"Thanks, my bill's in the mail," Jamie replied.

"See ya." He took off.

"Huh," Jamie muttered. "I never knew Drake was that—"

Sara grasped Jamie's wrist. Hard.

"What?" Jamie asked. "Are you taking my pulse?"

"I should." Sara's eyes were two huge, dark,

round pools of surprise. "Do you know what just happened?"

"We walked to school with a senior?" Jamie asked. "It was kind of fun, really, and—"

"Please shut up just a moment," Sara said. "This is important."

"What?"

"Jamie. You just had a perfectly normal, funny conversation with a really, really cute senior guy."

Jamie thought a minute. "I guess I did."

"You definitely did. You were amazing."

"I was?"

"Totally amazing!" Sara laughed. "What happened?"

"I have no idea," Jamie admitted. "I just . . . I forgot to be nervous, or something. Isn't that weird?"

"To tell you the truth," Sara said slowly, "it is, kind of."

Chapter

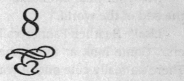

8

"*L*adies, please talk quietly until the substitute gym teacher arrives," the assistant principal announced, her voice echoing in the gymnasium.

"What luck," Lisa said, coming over to Jamie and Sara. "I definitely wasn't up for field hockey today."

"Me neither," Sara agreed. "Although it would be nice to be outside."

Lisa grinned at her. "Gee, could that be because the guys are outside running laps? And Jason's out there in his cute little gym shorts?"

"Possibly," Sara admitted. "I mean, we had such a fantastic time Saturday night, and—"

She stopped herself, cringing. "Sorry, Jamie. I didn't mean to remind you about—you know."

"Relax. I don't have a scarlet *B* on my chest. For Belch," Jamie said.

"Wow, you are taking it so well," Lisa marveled. "Because if it happened to me, I would, like, die."

"No, you, like, wouldn't," Jamie said. "It's not the end of the world."

"Lisa!" Heather Palmer called from the bleachers. "Come look at these photos from the dance. There's a really cute one of you and your ex."

"See you guys later," Lisa called, hurrying over to Heather.

"Oh, hey, I almost forgot," Jamie said. "I want to show you something." She unslung her backpack, unzipped it, and reached inside.

"Doughnuts? Pancakes? Waffles?" Sara joked. "Or maybe you've got your mom's homemade cookies in there?"

"Not food."

"What?"

"Hold on, I have to . . . here it is." Her fingers touched the smooth surface of the rock. She pulled it out of her bag and held it out to Sara.

"What is it? It's beautiful."

"Beats me," Jamie admitted. "I found it under my window. Stuck in a bush."

"Maybe it's a present from Nick," Sara ventured, "but he was afraid to ring your doorbell."

Jamie gave her friend an arch look. "Okay," Sara said quickly. "Bad guess. Can I touch it?"

"Sure. But first—"

Jamie walked over to a window so that the morning sun glinted off the Loverock. The light refracted through it, like a supercharged prism.

"That's incredible," Sara breathed. "Really."

"Here." Jamie handed it to her. Sara turned it over and over in her palm.

"Feel anything strange?"

"Strange like how?"

"Like . . . I don't know—that it's warm, or vibrating?" Jamie asked.

"Is this some kind of joke, Jam?"

"Nope. I asked you because whenever I hold it I feel this weird . . . thing."

" 'Thing,' " Sara echoed. "For a smart girl and a great writer, that was amazingly inarticulate."

"Like it's electric. Or giving off heat, or something," Jamie said. "You don't feel anything weird? Really?"

Sara shook her head and handed it back to Jamie. "Maybe only the person who finds it gets the buzz," Sara guessed, comically wriggling her eyebrows. "And it means extraterrestrials are going to beam you up to planet Big Burp, where—"

"Stop!" Jamie ordered, but she couldn't help laughing.

"Got another one for me?" Sara joked.

"If I had two of them, I'd give you the other one, and we'd both get beamed up to Big Burp," Jamie said.

"I'm touched."

"Yes, well, that's just the kind of wonderful friend I am," Jamie teased, batting her eyelashes. She looked down at the Loverock in the palm of her hand, and once again a tickle of vibration traveled up her arm. Weird. Really, really weird.

"You should show it to Mr. Benton," Sara suggested. "Maybe he'll know where it came from."

"Good idea," Jamie agreed. She dropped the Loverock into her backpack.

"Sara?"

"Hmmm?"

"Do you think—do you think Nick told all his friends about what happened?" Suddenly Jamie felt very insecure.

"He's not that kind of guy," Sara said firmly.

"If only I could do Saturday night over again. Wouldn't it be great if, when you really mess something up in your life, you could call 'do-over'? Like when we were ten and played jacks?"

Sara nodded. "We had fun back then, didn't we?"

"We did," Jamie agreed. "And we didn't have to worry about what boys thought of us, either."

And we didn't have to worry about ruining everything just because of one horrible mistake, Jamie added in her mind. *If only I could go to Nick and call: do-over.*

If only.

Chapter

9

"Most interesting. Most interesting, indeed."

Mr. Benton peered at the Loverock in his hands, turning it over and over just as Sara had. "I've never seen anything quite like it."

Jamie and Sara stood on the other side of his desk, waiting. They were between classes; this could not take long or they'd be late for English.

He frowned. "You said you bought this object where, Jamie?"

"I didn't buy it."

"No?"

"No," Jamie said. "I found it. Stuck in a thorn-bush, under my window."

"Strange," he said, "very strange."

"Why, Mr. Benton?" Sara asked. "Because of how it looks?"

"Or feels?" Jamie added. Maybe Mr. Benton would feel what she felt when she held it in her hands.

The elderly teacher turned Jamie's Loverock over and over again, pushing his glasses down to the end of his nose to examine it more closely.

"The texture is quite normal," Mr. Benton said. "Visually I find it aesthetically pleasing—quite lovely, really. But not particularly strange."

"Do you know what it's made of?" Jamie asked.

"I would say the main component appears to be silicon," Mr. Benton said. "It's quite common. The thing could have been fabricated at almost any good glass-blowing studio."

"You mean it isn't natural?" Jamie asked. For some reason, that surprised her.

"I wonder if perhaps . . ." The teacher's voice trailed off, and he stared into space for a moment or two. Sara checked her watch quickly, then shrugged at Jamie. If Mr. Benton didn't hurry, they were going to be late for their next class.

Mr. Benton looked at Jamie. "May I take a photograph of this?"

Jamie shrugged. "Sure."

Kids from Benton's next class, AP biology, drifted into the room. "Awesome," Dennis Wu said, peering at the Loverock. "What is that?"

"Exactly what we're trying to ascertain," the

teacher said. "It belongs to Jamie. What was it you called it, Jamie?"

"A Loverock," Jamie repeated, feeling a little silly. "Because, well, I guess because it's shaped like a heart." She shrugged again. "Somehow the word just came into my head."

Benton put the Loverock on his desk, took a small camera out of a drawer, and photographed the object from different angles. Then he did that staring thing again, tapping the tip of one finger thoughtfully against his lips.

"Uh, Mr. Benton?" Jamie finally said. "Sara and I are going to be late for—"

"Something is odd here." Mr. Benton didn't seem to hear what Jamie had just said. "I can't quite put my finger on it, but there's something peculiar." He picked up the Loverock and handed it to Jamie. "Well, we shall see what we shall see."

Whatever that means, Jamie thought.

She asked Mr. Benton for late passes for herself and Sara, which he wrote out. Then she put the Loverock back into her backpack and hustled off to English class.

"A Loverock?" Kate asked, turning it over in her hands.

"Yep," Jamie said. She leaned her elbows on the cafeteria table, across from Kate and Lisa.

Something had told her to show Kate the Loverock. Maybe it would distract Kate—or anyone else—from teasing her about Saturday night. So far, it was working.

In fact, no one in the cafeteria seemed to be looking oddly at Jamie, or whispering about her behind their hands, which meant that Nick hadn't told anyone what had happened.

That's what I call dodging a major bullet, Jamie thought. *It also means that Nick is just as wonderful as I thought he was. Because he kept his mouth shut. Still, I wonder who that girl was he was dancing with Saturday night.*

"Hey, Jam," Kate said, "are you sure some secret admirer didn't give you this as a gift?"

"Like I have a secret admirer," Jamie snorted. "Where's Sara?"

Kate smiled mischievously. "I think she's having lunch today with—speak of the devil." Just then Sara and Jason walked, side-by-side, into the cafeteria.

They look cute together, Jamie thought wistfully, *Sara with her dark hair and olive skin, and Jason, tall and rangy with blond hair. Like opposites attracting. Would Nick and I look that cute together? Not that I'll ever have the chance to find out.*

"Be right back," Jamie said. She had a sudden urge to go show Jason her Loverock.

"Hey, guys," Jamie said, sliding into a seat opposite them. "What's up?"

"Not much," Sara said. "We're having what passes for lunch."

"At least you're bright enough to go for the yogurt," Jason told her. He looked down at something brown and square-shaped inside a hamburger bun. "Am I taking my life in my hands by ingesting this?"

"Depends on how strong your stomach is," Jamie said. "I wouldn't worry too much, though. Just because last year a bunch of seniors who ate that all ended up barfing their guts out in study hall—"

"Get outta here," Jason scoffed, but clearly he wasn't completely sure whether or not Jamie was teasing him or telling the truth.

"Well, they recycled it for this year," Jamie went on. "So probably whatever organisms made everyone sick have died by now. Looks dee-lish."

After a beat, Jason burst out laughing. He pushed his lunch tray away from him. "Funny how I just lost my appetite."

"Here." Sara fed him a spoonful of strawberry yogurt.

"Decent, but I think I hear a bag of chips calling to me," Jason said. "Be right back."

As soon as Jason was out of hearing range, Sara leaned over the table toward Jamie. "Isn't he fantastic? He asked if we could have lunch together."

"Great," Jamie said. She plucked a grape off the small bunch on Sara's tray. "I'm really happy for you."

"Well, it's the first time I ever . . . you know, really liked a guy who really liked me back." Sara nibbled at her lower lip. "My parents could be a problem, though. They think I shouldn't date until I'm about thirty."

"Don't call it 'dating,' then," Jamie advised. "That's one of those parental red-flag words, especially for your parents. Call it 'hanging out.' "

"Ah, salt, grease, and potatoes, what could be better?" Jason slid back into the seat next to Sara, chomping on a mouthful of chips.

"While you're clogging your arteries, check this out," Jamie said. She took the Loverock off her lap and held it out to Jason.

"What is it?"

"Just something that Sara made in her spare time, she's quite the artist," Jamie said. "She also holds the world record in the women's two-hundred-meter dash, and is singing a duet with Ani DiFranco on her next CD."

Jason turned to Sara. "Jamie ought to be your publicist."

"Oh, I already pay her to say nice things about me," Sara joked.

"And does she return the favor?" Jamie asked. "No, she does not. But for the tiniest crumb of a compliment—"

"What?" Sara asked, wide-eyed. "I always say nice—"

"Joke," Jamie interrupted.

"Seriously, though," Jason said. "What is that thing?"

Jamie looked at it glittering in the palm of her hand. "My pet Loverock."

"Do you have to water and feed it?" Jason asked, reaching for another chip.

"And diaper it," Jamie added, making a face. "How else can we ensure that there will be another generation of little Loverocks?"

Jason laughed. "And how do two people make a little Loverock?"

Jamie shook her head and sighed. "It's sad, really, when a guy of fifteen still doesn't know where little Loverocks come from."

She pushed her chair back and stood up. "I think it's best if Sara explains the facts of life to you, Jason. So I'll just be over there"—she pointed to Kate and Lisa on the other side of the cafeteria—"in case you have any other questions. Bye!"

Jamie was on her way back to Kate and Lisa when she saw Nick come into the cafeteria with Alan and two girls. The girls were really cute cheerleader types. In fact, one of them was the girl Nick had been dancing with on Saturday night.

Seeing Nick made her heart do a few fancy trampoline tricks. But it didn't matter anymore. Nick was with . . . whoever that girl was. And Jamie knew she couldn't call do-over.

"Hi, Jamie," Nick said as he walked by Jamie with his friends.

"Hi," Jamie called back. She waited for the familiar bile in her stomach to well up, for her hands to get all clammy and cold; basically, for a mini-panic attack. And waited. And waited.

But it didn't happen.

Huh. Maybe I didn't freak out because I know I already blew it with him, Jamie thought as she sat back down with her friends.

"What did you say to Jason that made him laugh like that?" Lisa asked Jamie. "We could see it all the way over here."

"I don't remember." Jamie picked up her cheese sandwich, then put it down again.

She hadn't had any trouble talking with Drake— a senior—on the way to school that morning.

She'd just had a normal, funny conversation with Jason.

And now she'd said hello to Nick without feeling like she was going to hurl.

Something very strange was going on.

Very, very strange.

E-mail
From: 15Jamiesworld
To: 14ZZZDreamer
Re: The Rock

Matt, I've logged on very little lately, and I'm really sorry. I've been spending a lot of time with my friends, and something pretty embarrassing happened to me at the school dance, which maybe I'll be able to tell you about by the time I'm forty, and maybe not. But I did want to tell you about this really weird thing I found outside my window, stuck in one of our bushes. I don't know how to describe it, so I've taken a picture of it and fed it into the scanner. I'm going to send you the file so you can look at it. What do you think it is?

E-mail
From: 14ZZZDreamer
To: 15Jamiesworld
Re: Your photo

Jamie, gotta run, am between classes. Got your e-mail. As for that pic you sent: beats me!!!! Funny thing is, I had something incredibly embarrassing happen to me over the weekend, too. Maybe by the time I'm fifty I'll be able to tell you about it. And maybe not. Every time I think of it I don't know whether to laugh or cry.

Chapter

10

MEMORANDUM

From: Dr. Robert Benton, Science Teacher, LaGrange High
School, LaGrange, La.
To: Professor Kari Eskwitt, United States Geological
Survey, Washington, D.C.
Re: Glassy object reported

Dear Dr. Eskwitt,
Your memorandum to the principal of my
high school was posted, as you requested, in the
teachers' lounge. That memo asked that, as part
of the USGS's ongoing research efforts, any and
all odd-shaped objects that could conceivably be
natural formations be reported to your office.

I write to report that such an object may have come to my attention.

One of my students, Jamie Dobrin, brought to my office earlier this week a glassy-looking object the size of a softball, but the shape of a valentine. I photographed this object, and a copy of that photo is enclosed. At first glance I assumed that the object was man-made. On further examination—there is a striking pattern on the object that would seem to be the result of its being exposed to extreme friction-based heat—I have come to believe that the object is not man-made.

Here is what is also striking to me: I am the faculty adviser to the school's Horatio Alger Society, a club that offers special attention, tutoring, and mentoring to those students who face special challenges but are particularly committed to the academic process.

As adviser, I keep a clippings file of magazine and newspaper stories that I feel could be meaningful to my advisees.

When Ms. Dobrin brought this object to me, it troubled me immediately. And then I remembered why. It was because of an article I had clipped recently from the *Times-Picayune* about another New Orleans–area teen, a poor girl named Marilee Ellis, who claimed to have been given a similar object by her grandmother before winning the Louisiana Lotto.

As I seem to have a talent for remembering minute details that no one cares about, something about that stuck in my mind. To wit: In a follow-up story that I also clipped, Ellis refers to her object as a Loverock.

I asked Ms. Dobrin if she knew Ms. Ellis, and she claims that she does not. This appeared to be a truthful statement on her part. Besides, I can't think of any motivation she might have to lie. Yet both these young women possess objects that each calls a "Loverock."

While this evidence is more anecdotal than scientific, I did feel that it warranted bringing to your attention. I should be pleased to be kept informed as to the results of whatever investigation you do.

HART BENTON
LaGrange High School, LaGrange, LA

"I should be pleased to be kept informed as to the results of whatever investigation you do. Hart Benton, LaGrange High School, LaGrange, Louisiana."

Dr. Louise Warner, chief of the Substance Z recovery project, laid the memo down on her desk and studied each grave face staring back at her.

There were no windows in the conference room. It was located a hundred feet underground in the most secure building at a military base outside of New Orleans. The only light in the room was artificial and gave a greenish cast to the skin of the assembled Substance Z team.

Dr. Ivar Chambul, one of the lead scientists, whistled a low note. "Well, there it is. Another girl with a chunk of Substance Z. In LaGrange, where we're already concentrating our efforts. Let's get to work and see how the Sub Z affects her, and whether she goes through the Mirror Image Effect."

At his usual seat at the far end of the table, Dr. Austin Leo cleared his throat loudly. All eyes at the table swung to him. Leo was old enough to be some of the scientists' grandfather, and he was brilliant. Very difficult to be around, yes. Iconoclastic, yes. But brilliant.

It had been Dr. Leo's theoretical work that had led the Defense Department to undertake the Substance Z project in the first place: to attempt to create a super-weapon that would turn well-trained enemy forces into their precise opposites, and thus render such forces impotent.

No one had planned for the satellite containing experimental Substance Z to be knocked out of the sky by a stray meteor, and no one had planned for it to burst into pieces over the greater New Orleans area.

What had happened since was extremely troubling. Various fifteen-year-old girls in the New Orleans area had found or been given pieces of Substance Z. And each girl had experienced the transformative Mirror Image Effect.

So many questions were unanswered: Why only teenage girls? Why were all the pieces of Sub Z heart-shaped? What would the long-term effect be on these girls?

They were the top scientific minds in the country. And yet, none of them had the answers.

Dr. Leo pounded the table with a closed fist, and the rest of the team jumped. "Don't you people have a shred of decency?"

"What do you mean, Austin?" Dr. Warner asked him.

"I mean, now we've got the United States Geological Survey sending utterly misleading memos to high school science teachers, for pity's sake. We've got high school science teachers spying on their students."

"Please calm down, Dr. Leo," Dr. Warner advised, her voice low. "We need cool heads here."

"Well, too bad for that!" Dr. Leo shouted. "Because I am anything but cool, Louise. What are we going to allow next? Search warrants to enter the homes of every young person in the South?"

"Dr. Leo, please—"

"Haven't you heard of something called the Fourth Amendment? What is it we think we're doing here?"

"We are doing the best we can," Dr. Chambul replied. "We do not want to trample on anyone's civil rights. However, the security of the United States could be at stake, here."

"How Machiavellian of us," Dr. Leo sneered. "We say we can do whatever we want because we have a greater good in mind."

Dr. Warner clasped her hands together. "So, just what do you propose, Dr. Leo?"

"That we just leave the rest of them alone. We've seen the Mirror Image Effect in three young people thus far. The effect is profound, but benign. We know what we need to know."

"That's not possible, Austin," Dr. Warner said softly. "Our order to follow and study any and all people we positively identify as having been exposed to Substance Z comes from the highest possible levels. *The highest.*"

"Yes, yes, top, top, double secret and all that." Dr. Leo stood, stretching his gaunt frame to its full six-foot, two-inch height. "But you mark my words," he added. "We'll be sorry for all this, someday. We'll be very sorry." Then, without a backward glance, he stormed out of the conference room.

Chapter

11

"*That* outfit is very cute," Jamie told Cerise as the two of them stopped to look in the window of a new boutique at the New Orleans Centre mall. The mannequin in the window display wore a pretty red sweater with pink hearts on it, and her jeans had pink and red ribbons sewn around the bottoms.

Cerise shrugged. "A little too precious for my taste, thanks."

Jamie, who was wearing khakis and a little Lycra stretch shirt, took in her older sister's thrift-store paisley baggy pants and men's bowling shirt that read "Fred" on the pocket. As for makeup, Cerise wore some heavy liquid black eyeliner, but nothing else.

"If you had a date, you'd dress differently, wouldn't you?" Jamie asked.

"Please," Cerise scoffed. "Why would I change how I like to dress just because I'm gonna be with a guy? Besides, I don't believe in 'dating.' It's totally artificial."

"But you've had so many boyfriends," Jamie reminded her.

"That's because I don't date."

Well, I'd like to experience it at least once before I reject it, Jamie thought as she and her sister started strolling along again. Cerise had come to the mall to pick up some old vinyl records for her collection, and Jamie had asked if she could tag along. After all, they hardly ever spent any time together. She was hoping that maybe Cerise could give her some big-sister-type advice about guys.

"So, if you don't believe in dating, how do you get to know a guy you like?" Jamie asked her sister.

"Just like you get to know anyone. You talk to each other. Do stuff as a group. Like that. Hey, let's go in this store—they've got those gauze skirts from India on sale."

"Don't you already own, like, six of those skirts?" Jamie asked.

Cerise didn't bother to answer her; she just disappeared inside.

"Hey, Cerise, I'll meet you down at Finyl Vinyl!" Jamie called to her sister.

"Whatever," Cerise called back, already pawing through a barrel of sale items.

Jamie kept walking, taking her time, enjoying window-shopping. And, she had to admit, she was enjoying looking at the cute guys who roamed the mall in packs.

"Hey, that girl is hot!" Jamie heard a girl's voice. "Isn't that Jamie Dobrin?"

Jamie looked away from the window of Threads, the clothing store, and toward the voice. Kate and Ben were walking toward her, holding hands.

"Cruising for studs?" Kate asked Jamie.

"Why bother, when one is right in front of me?" Jamie replied. "You don't mind having stud status, do you, Ben?"

Ben scratched his chin. "Not sure what that means."

"Oh, you know," Jamie began. "Cute, fine, hot, the kind of guy a girl dreams about at night. That kind of thing."

Ben looked both embarrassed and flattered. "I think I can handle that."

"Well, handle it in this direction," Kate told him. She turned back to Jamie. "Are you feeling all right?"

"Sure. Why?"

"We can talk about it later. I'll call you."

"Sure," Jamie agreed, starting to walk away.

Then she turned back to them. "Oh, Ben? One last thing. If I dream about you, it won't be my fault. I mean, we don't have any control over our dreams."

"Yeah," Ben agreed, walking backward so that he could keep focusing on Jamie.

Kate yanked him around to face her. Not exactly subtle.

Oh well, Jamie thought. *She'll get over it. After all, I was only fooling around. No. I was flirting. Flirting. With Kate's boyfriend. And it just kind of . . . happened.*

She caught her own reflection in the Threads window. Nice hair pulled back in a messy ponytail. Cute enough, but not some raving beauty. She didn't look any different from the way she had last week. So what had made her flirt with Ben like that?

A brain tumor.

That's what flew into Jamie's mind. She recalled that in her psychology class, Lerner had told them that depending on where a brain tumor was located, it could cause severe personality changes.

So was it possible that she had a—

Stop thinking like that, she scolded herself. *Maybe you're just getting more mature. Which is long overdue.*

She decided to stop in the bookstore to get a novel Sara had recommended.

What was the name of it? Something about a heart.

She was lost in thought, head down, trying to

remember the book's title, when she bumped into something.

She looked up. Correction. Bumped into *someone*. And, like some nightmare replaying itself, the someone turned out to be Nick Brooks.

"We can't go on meeting like this," Jamie blurted out. Nick smiled.

"Buying a good book?" Jamie asked as if talking to Nick in a bookstore was the most natural thing in the world. As if she didn't dream about him kissing her and—

Nick held up a paperback. Jamie read the cover. *"The Heart Is a Lonely Hunter*—that's it!"

"That's what?" Nick asked, confused.

"The book Sara told me to read," Jamie said eagerly. "By Carson McCullers, right? Sara said it's great."

"It's on Dunbar's optional reading list. I'm this close to nailing an A in his class," Nick said, holding up his thumb and forefinger.

Jamie's eyebrows went up. "No kidding? I heard he's the toughest English teacher at the school. My sister told me he wouldn't give her more than a B on any paper she wrote, no matter what."

"Maybe Cerise is a B-level writer," Nick suggested.

Jamie laughed. "Now that you mention it."

He cocked his head at her. "You seem, I don't know, different today."

"I had a personality transplant Sunday," Jamie

said, straight-faced. "It's amazing what they can do with laser surgery these days." Nick chuckled.

"Did you know that you have dimples when you laugh?" Jamie asked.

"Uh . . . no."

"Well, you do," Jamie said. "And they are very, very cute, in a young Tom Cruise kind of way."

"Uh . . . thanks."

"Uh, you're welcome," Jamie quipped.

"Well, I have to go meet my big sister," Nick began.

"You have an older sister, too?" Jamie asked. "I didn't know that. Mine thinks she's Woodstock Nation reincarnated. How about yours?"

"Marci's just kind of studious, I guess. She's working for a year before she starts law school."

"I'll remember that next time I'm committing grand theft auto," Jamie joked.

"Well, I have to go," Nick said. "So, see ya."

"See ya," Jamie said easily. "Oh, call me if you want. I'd love to hear what you think of that book."

"Okay," Nick said. Then he disappeared around the corner.

Oh, my gosh, did that really just happen? Jamie wondered. Little bubbles of happiness were pop-pop-popping all over her skin. *It did! I know it did.*

"I just flirted with Nick Brooks," Jamie whispered, wrapping her arms around herself. "And it was fun."

* * *

"Hey, Cerise, notice any resemblance to my older sister?" Jamie held up the cover of an old Janis Joplin album she'd pulled out of a rack at Finyl Vinyl.

"Beats looking like Patsi Preppie," Cerise muttered, looking through a stack of old records.

"What, that's what you think I look like, you mean?"

"If the khakis fit, et cetera."

Jamie folded her arms. "Labels are silly. I thought you hated people who label people." Cerise shrugged and kept thumbing through the albums.

"Well, terrif," Jamie said. "I'm so glad we've had this sister-to-sister bonding moment."

Behind her, someone laughed. A girl with a hip alternative look, dressed in black pants and a pink-and-black zebra-striped T-shirt, grinned at her.

"Sorry," the girl said. "I couldn't help overhearing you. It's just that you sounded just like I sound with my sister. She's the beauty pageant type. And I'm . . . not."

But you could be if you wanted to be, Jamie thought.

Whoever this girl was, Jamie thought she was just beautiful, in a totally original way. And she looked familiar, too.

"Do I know you?" Jamie asked her.

"Dunno. Do you?"

"It's just that you seem familiar to me," Jamie explained.

"Probably that." The girl cocked her chin toward

a poster of herself, surrounded by vinyl records. It was an advertisement for the store.

"You're a model!" Jamie exclaimed.

"No, not really," the girl said. "Turns out it's not my thing. I'm Callie Bailey." She stuck her hand out and Jamie shook it.

"Jamie Dobrin. Ouch!"

She pulled her hand away from Callie's, because she'd just gotten an electric shock up her arm.

"Did you feel that?" they both asked at once. Then they both laughed.

"This is kinda weird," Callie said.

Jamie nodded. "Don't you need some kind of conductor for static electricity?"

"To tell you the truth, science is one of my many short suits," Callie admitted. She studied Jamie a moment. "You know, now that you mention it, something about you seems familiar to me, too. Where do you live?"

"LaGrange."

"That's not it, then," Callie mused. "But I just have this weird feeling." She laughed. "This is going to sound crazy, but I'm having a déjà vu moment."

"Like you and I had this conversation before?" Jamie asked.

"Almost," Callie said. Jamie could see that Callie was racking her mind to figure it out. Suddenly Callie snapped her fingers. "Marilee."

"Pardon me?"

"When I met Marilee Ellis!" Callie exclaimed. "That's when I had this exact same weird feeling."

"Who's she?" Jamie asked.

"She's— oof!" Callie fell over, pushed from behind. And she was dripping with Coke.

"I'm so sorry," a young woman said to her. "I broke my glasses and I lost my contact lenses and . . . did I hurt you?" she asked as she helped Callie up.

"No." Callie looked down at her dripping wet clothes. "I'm kind of a sticky mess, though."

"Listen, that was all my fault," the young woman said. "I'm completely to blame. Let me buy you a new shirt."

"No, no, you don't have to do that," Callie said, squeezing the Coke out of her hair.

"I insist," the young woman said. "My mom owns that new boutique at the other end of the mall. We can go down there and you can pick something out. In fact, my mom has some really cute stretchy T-shirts on sale—kind of like the one you have on, but printed with Asian scenes."

"I still don't think—"

"I'm going to feel terrible if you don't," the girl said. "And I know you don't want to leave me with a lifetime of guilt."

"Well . . ." Callie wavered.

"Good, then it's settled. Let's go," the girl said.

Callie turned to Jamie. "Wanna come with?"

"Jam, we're leaving the mall as soon as I pay for these," Cerise said, overhearing Callie.

"I guess that means the answer is no," Jamie said, making a face. "Six months and twenty-three days until I can get my driver's license."

"Tell me about it," Callie sympathized.

"I don't mean to rush you," the girl said, "but my mom's closing early today, so—"

"Jam, we've got to get going. Straight home," Cerise told her sister.

"Well, it was nice meeting you, Jamie," Callie said, walking away from her backward.

But we didn't just meet. We already know each other, Jamie thought. Which was a totally bizarre, out-there thought, and not one she was about to say out loud. So she waved goodbye and kept her mouth shut.

The young woman hurrying away from the record store heaved a secret sigh of relief. Her mother didn't own a store at the mall. And she hadn't spilled her Coke on Callie by mistake.

But as a member of the Substance Z Field Team, it was her responsibility to avert possible disaster.

Callie and Jamie both had found Loverocks.

And the connection between them was one the scientists wanted to study and understand while it was still possible. It was bad enough that Callie had met Marilee. And knew that Marilee had a Loverock.

Now this.

The Substance Z team had recently been instructed from the highest level of government to do whatever to keep the Loverock girls apart.

A spilled Coke and the price of a new shirt had seemed like a small price to pay.

Chapter

12

"Voilà! How does this look?" Jamie asked. She held her homemade kite up for Sara to see; Sara appraised it carefully.

"I think it's fabulous," Sara pronounced. "I really love how you put sparkles all around your name."

"Yes, my name in lights. How perfect," Jamie teased.

Jamie, with her dad's help, had made a huge bat-shaped kite out of clear plastic sheeting attached to clear plastic bracing rods. The idea was to make the kite see-through. Then, she'd written her own name with glittery silver paint in thick letters across the plastic.

The kite had a wing-span of five feet. It was enormous. It was monstrous. It was impossible to miss.

Jamie and Sara were going to the annual La-Grange Airborne Festival, a major event that was held on the LaGrange Green, at the municipal park out behind the high school. People of all ages came to the green with kites and model airplanes. And, of course, there was also a huge crowd of spectators, attracted by free food and sodas as well as by various contests.

Jamie looked over at Sara's kite, an old-fashioned diamond-shaped one in the national colors of Mexico. The tail, instead of just being a rag with knots tied in it, had tiny Mexican sombreros attached.

"Tell me the truth," Jamie began, "did your parents blackmail you into going with the Mexico thing?"

Sara laughed. "No. But you can imagine how happy they were when they saw it."

Jamie studied her friend a moment. "Don't you ever . . . don't you ever get tired of being perfect, Sara?"

"Me, perfect? I'm so far from perfect that—"

"You know what I mean," Jamie insisted. "You always do exactly what your parents want you to do."

Sara fingered the tail of her kite. "Maybe because I know how much my older brother and sister hurt them. I guess I feel kind of like I have to make up for them."

Jamie hugged her. "You don't have to make up for anything, Sara. They're them and you're you."

"Thank you, O Wise One," Sara replied regally. "And where did you acquire such mythic wisdom, might I ask?"

"I owe it all to my Loverock," Jamie replied.

Sara groaned. "You and that Loverock again. Has Benton said anything else to you about it?"

"Nope. Still waiting."

"Well, my advice about your Loverock is: Find a better object of your affections."

"Like Nick?"

"Right on the first guess," Sara said. She reached over and picked up Jamie's Loverock from the nightstand. "O, Great Loverock, make Nick fall madly in love with Jamie."

"Amazing."

"What?" Sara put the Loverock back on the nightstand.

"How quickly that worked. Because guess who had an actual conversation with Nick Brooks?"

Sara picked up Jamie's hairbrush and began to brush her thick, dark hair. "My first guess is . . . you?"

Jamie nodded. "I ran into him at the mall."

"Don't tell me. He belched at you this time."

"Incorrect."

Sara knocked the back of Jamie's brush against the bottom of her sneaker. "Let me see—you got so nervous when you saw him that you faked an intense toothache and ran home, and then wrote an article for the 'zine about it?"

"Incorrect again, my dear. I, Jamie Dobrin, had an actual conversation with Nick Brooks. I ran into him at the bookstore. And I didn't write a 'zine article, either. I didn't feel like it. It was weird."

"So?" Sara asked.

"The thing is, I didn't have any trouble talking to him," Jamie said. "It was as if I was talking online to my friend Matt in Wisconsin—that's how easy it was."

"What did you do, pretend Nick was Matt?"

Jamie shook her head. "I'm telling you, I didn't do anything. It was like I just had this—I don't know—this flirting power all of a sudden. Does that sound crazy?"

"Yes, actually, it does," Sara said. "Except the other morning, when we walked to school, you kind of flirted with Drake, remember? And when you were with Jason in the cafeteria—"

"I wasn't flirting with Jason," Jamie protested. "I would never flirt with your boyfriend."

"Well, you did. A little. I didn't mind, though, Jam. I figured you were just practicing."

Guilt washed over Jamie. Because in her heart she knew she had flirted with Jason. At least a little.

"These are going to be the two best ones there," Sara said, changing the subject.

"We win the multicultural and garish awards, anyway," Jamie said. "Hey, you think Nick will be at the Green?"

"Sure," Sara said. "Everyone will be there, just like every other year."

"But last year Nick and I weren't—whatever it is we are." Jamie hurried over to the mirror. "Does my hair look okay? Should I change shirts? Do you have any lip gloss?" Sara stared at her as if she had just sprouted wings.

"What?" Jamie asked.

"Do you hear yourself?"

"What's wrong with wanting to look nice, in case I run into Nick?"

"Nothing," Sara said, her voice low. "Forget it." She peered at the little sombreros on her kite—they looked as if they could use another shot of quick-drying glue. She carefully added tiny dots of glue from the glue stick.

"Sara?" Jamie asked.

"Hmmm?"

"I'm serious. Do you have some lip gloss I can use?"

Mr. Dobrin helped Jamie and Sara unload their gear at LaGrange Green. Then he shut the back hatch of the Explorer. "Okay, you two. Have a blast."

"Thanks for the ride, Dad." Jamie kissed her father's cheek. "And for the help."

Her father gave her a quick hug. "I only wish I could stay and watch you fly it, honey. But Cerise asked me days ago if I'd help her edit some big paper she's writing. And I haven't had any time to do it, so—"

"It's all right," Jamie said. "I understand."

Her father smiled ruefully. "Your sister hasn't asked me to help her with—well, pretty much anything—since junior high. So I'd better take advantage of the opportunity. I'll pick you up at . . . five. How's that?"

"Fine, Dad."

"Thanks, Mr. Dobrin," Sara said.

They waved goodbye as the Explorer drove off, then gathered up their kites and kite string, and headed into the park.

A marvelous sight awaited them: several hundred kites, of all shapes and sizes, flying against a crisp blue sky in brisk, fifteen-mile-per-hour south winds. The breeze was so fresh that Jamie thought she could smell salt air from the not-far-off Gulf of Mexico.

"Wow!" Sara exclaimed. "This is amazing."

"Absolutely," Jamie agreed. "Every year I get psyched about it as if it's the very first time."

"I know what you mean," Sara agreed.

"Hey, there's Jason." Jamie pointed to a small rise, where Jason was flying his kite with another guy Jamie didn't know.

"He's with his friend Shawn, from Overton," Sara said. "You know him?"

Jamie shook her head.

"He's a junior, their dads work together," Sara explained.

"Is he cute?" Jamie asked offhandedly. "I can't tell from here."

"Is that all you care about all of a sudden?"

"No. First I care if he can walk and chew gum at the same time. Then I care if he's cute," Jamie joked. "Come on. Let's go give them a surprise."

The guys were flying their kites about a hundred yards downwind from them. Jason's kite looked like one of the dangerous water moccasin snakes that lived in the bayous. His friend, Shawn, had brought an old-fashioned box kite. Jamie quickly noticed that Shawn was definitely cute. Highly cute, even. His brown hair was cut short, and he had big blue eyes and broad shoulders.

Jason was really happy to see them, and quickly introduced Jamie to Shawn. "Hey," Shawn said easily, keeping an eye on his kite.

"Hey, yourself," Jamie said in a teasing voice. She quickly got her contraption up in the air.

"Wow!" Sara said as she unspooled string. "That's so fabulous. All you can see is your name! Here goes mine."

Sara started running, and Jamie and the guys followed. The stiff breeze kept their kites flying high. "They're awfully close to one another," Sara pointed out. "We could end up with kite-string spaghetti up there."

"Can I help it if my kite is attracted to his kite?" Jamie asked.

"Which 'his' are you talking about?" Jason asked.

"Wouldn't you like to know," Jamie replied. "Hey, watch your line." She glanced over at Shawn. "So, you go to Overton High?"

Shawn nodded. "It's pretty cool."

"Didn't some girl at your school win the lottery?" Sara asked. "I remember something."

"Marilee Ellis," Shawn filled in. "Lucky, huh?"

"No kidding," Jamie agreed.

The four of them stood together until a gust of wind pulled Jamie's kite and Jason's snake off to one side. The two of them edged to the left, trying to control them. "No, no, no, you stupid snake!" Jamie yelled into the sky. "Stay away from my flying namesake."

"My snake appears to have a mind of its own," Jason replied.

"Who was your model? Chris Morland?" Jamie joked.

Chris Morland was the captain of the LaGrange High School wrestling team. He'd also been in and out of juvie and rehab several times. He wasn't exactly considered a model citizen.

Jason laughed. "No. But if I'd thought of it, I'd have put Morland's face on it. Then no one would dare get near my kite."

"Feel free to do it next year," Jamie offered as she reeled in some line. "Then let go of the string, so it takes off for Nebraska, or something. Which is what the whole school would like Chris to do."

"Except Nebraska doesn't want him," Jason said.

"Good point." Jamie thought a moment. "We'll have to throw something into the deal. Maybe a few great jazz musicians from the French Quarter. How's that?"

"Ask Nebraska," Jason said. He regarded Jamie thoughtfully. "Don't take this wrong, Jamie, but I had absolutely no idea that you were so . . . well, so cool."

"See what you've been missing?"

"I'm serious," Jason said. "I can see why Sara likes you so much."

"And I can see why Sara likes you so much," Jamie replied flirtatiously. It just popped out of her mouth.

"Actually, I'd like to get a chance to know you even better." He moved closer to Jamie.

He's definitely flirting back, Jamie realized. *And I have to admit, having such a cute guy flirt with me is fun. I'm sure he knows it doesn't mean anything. Well, pretty sure, anyway.*

Sara walked over to them, carefully guiding her kite. "You guys looked like you were deep in conversation."

"Talking about Chris Morland, believe it or not," Jamie told her. "Uh-oh, looks like Shawn's is crashing."

Near where Shawn was struggling to keep his kite aloft, Jamie saw Nick. Her heart immediately did that Nick-is-around thing. No other guy made her feel that way. He was with a little girl, who was trying—and not succeeding—at getting a kite into the air.

"Who's the girl? Nick's little sister?" Jamie asked her friends.

"Yeah," Jason said. "Cute, huh?"

"If you mean Nick, then the answer is yes," Jamie murmured.

"You into him?" Jason asked.

"Um—he's just a friend," Jamie replied carefully.

"A friend?" Sara echoed incredulously.

"Right," Jamie said. "It's not like we— Oops, Shawn's is down."

"I'll go help him with it," Sara offered. "Unless you'd rather go, Jason?"

"No, that's cool, you can go," Jason said.

"Oh. Okay." Sara took off, glancing back at Jason and Jamie over her shoulder.

"Good," Jason said. He let out some kite string, so his kite soared higher. "So listen, Jamie, maybe sometime we could do something together."

"Define 'something,' " Jamie suggested.

He laughed. "Hang out, I mean."

Is Jason asking me out? On a date? Is that what he means by "hang out"?

"But what about Sara?" Jamie asked, her antennae instantly alerted.

"Sara's great. We're still getting to know each other," Jason said easily. "The way that you and I are getting to know each other. That's cool, right?"

"Uh . . ."

She didn't know what to say.

Jason wants to hang out with me. That means he thinks it's cool to be seen with me. And he's one of the coolest, hottest, most popular guys in the entire school. But Sara loves him. And Sara is my best friend.

"We could hang out sometime," Jamie finally said. "Like, maybe me and Nick and you and Sara."

"Is that how it is?" Jason asked, his voice low.

"Listen Jason, I—"

"I haven't even ever gone out with Sara yet."

"I know. But she really likes you, you know. I know for a fact that she's already fantasizing about what it would be like to kiss you."

"And just how do you know that?"

"Maybe I'll whisper how I know in your ear sometime," Jamie said.

Jason moved even closer. "How about now?"

"How about I'm going to go talk to Nick?" Jamie moved deftly away from him. "It was great talking with you, Jason," she added. "Really great."

"Right back atcha," Jason agreed.

Her kite still flying, her name emblazoned in silver letters against the sky, Jamie headed for Nick Brooks.

She couldn't see Jason, still standing where she'd left him, both hands on the kite string, staring at her with something very close to longing.

She also couldn't see the three members of the Substance Z reconnaissance team who had followed her father's van to LaGrange Green. They were posing as members of the crowd, while what they actually were doing was following Jamie's every move with highly sensitive, hidden equipment.

Videotaping every movement—and recording her every word.

Chapter

13

&

The annual LaGrange High School–versus–Belleville High School football game was always the seventh game of the season. The two schools had been rivals for nearly fifty years, and, even though they were separated by nearly twenty miles, both the game and the postgame parties were always attended by students from both schools.

The two schools were rivals who played hard but always respected each other. This year's game was no exception. Belleville held the lead until late in the fourth quarter, when LaGrange thrilled the home crowd—including Jamie and all her friends— by driving the length of the field and scoring a touchdown to win by a single point.

Jamie had cheered her lungs out. The game was such a blast that Jamie couldn't imagine how Kate's big postgame party could be any more fun.

"L-A-G-R-A-N-G-E!" The chanting started at one side of Kate's big backyard, with its heated pool full of kids, and spread to the other side.

"We *are* Belleville!" answered a huge group of Belleville students who were also at the party. The good-natured chanting went back and forth for quite a while, loud enough to be heard over the hip-hop that blared from outdoor speakers.

Jamie sat on the edge of the pool, dunking her bare feet in the warm water and nibbling on a plate of nachos. She was lost in thought as the party cranked up around her. *Everyone seems to be here except Nick,* she mused, scanning the crowd for him. It looked as if he hadn't shown up. Jamie couldn't help but feel disappointed.

When I saw him at the kite festival, she remembered, *all he did was say hello to me—mumble it, really—and then make some excuse about having to watch his sister. I don't understand. If he likes me, then why won't he—*

"Hey." Lisa's new boyfriend, Scott, plopped down next to her. "Great party, huh?"

"It's fantastic," Jamie said happily. "Hey, speaking of great, where's the great Lisa?"

Scott shrugged. "I think she went to comb her hair or something."

"Some people do that," Jamie joked, her voice deep

and scratchy. She laughed. "I'm so hoarse from yelling I sound like I have a cold. Or like that actress from the forties with the sultry voice—what was her name?"

"Lauren Bacall," Scott said. "I'm a serious old-movie buff. Come to think of it, you do kind of sound like her right now. Sexy."

Jamie looked at him through half-lowered eyes. "You think?"

"Absolutely. You need to yell more often."

"Well, I'll keep that in mind." She smiled at him.

"Killer smile," Scott told her.

"Thanks." She gave him a sultry look. "I'll settle for merely injuring you, though. Death seems a little extreme."

He put his hands over his heart in mock pain. "Ouch."

Just then, Jamie saw Lisa on the other side of the pool. She'd changed into a cute pink bikini. Jamie waved to her.

"Scott!" Lisa shouted across the pool. "Come swimming with me?"

"Nah," he said. "I just ate."

Jamie laughed. "I don't think she wanted you to swim the English Channel with her. You could risk it."

"Except that I'd rather sit here with you," Scott said, his voice low. "That a problem?"

"I love talking with you," Jamie replied, "but—"

"Later, Lees," Scott called to her. "I'm busy with Jamie."

A bunch of kids had heard the exchange, and

they snickered. Meanwhile, Lisa's jaw fell open. Her boyfriend had just dissed her in front of everyone. Just so he could hang out with Jamie. Jamie, of all people.

Jamie saw Lisa's reaction. *But I didn't do anything,* she thought. *I was sitting here, and he sat down.*

Jamie jumped to her feet. "Look, Scott. Go swimming with Lisa. I've got to . . . go find Sara," she invented.

He reached for her wrist. "Later, maybe?"

"You never know what could happen later," she replied, her voice full of promise. Scott's face lit up.

Why did I say that? Jamie wondered. *I certainly didn't mean to imply that Scott and I would get together. Well, I can't help it if he jumps to the wrong conclusion.*

"Go swimming with your *girlfriend*," Jamie said pointedly. "Catch you later."

"Hope so," Scott called to her as she hurried off.

Jamie made her way through the big crowd and onto the back patio. There, dozens of kids were dancing to Lauryn Hill. Jamie bopped to the music, watching the crowd.

"Dance, Jamie?"

Kate's latest boyfriend, Ben, stood towering over her. He was more than six feet tall, and was clad in jeans and a retro fifties kind of sports shirt. He had black hair and blue eyes and the face of a movie star.

Kate is so beautiful, Jamie thought. *But Ben might be even better-looking than she is.*

"I'd love to dance!" Jamie shouted as the music cranked up a notch. Ben put out his hand, which Jamie took, and then followed him directly into the center of the pulsating crowd.

As the beat pounded, Jamie lost herself in the throbbing music. And then, when the tempo changed, and Mary Chapin Carpenter's voice began a slow country waltz, she willingly stepped into Ben's outstretched arms.

After all, it's just a dance, she told herself.

Jamie felt Ben's hand circle the small of her back, gently caressing her. She let her cheek rest against Ben's well-muscled shoulder. Her eyes closed, as together they floated in a world of their own.

"Mmmmm," Ben murmured. "Don't you feel good."

She opened her eyes to smile up at him. But instead, she noticed Kate staring at them from the back screen door. *Oops*, Jamie thought. *I don't want her to think that I'm stealing her boyfriend, because it was Ben who—*

She pushed herself gently away from Ben. "Excuse me," she said, "but I've got to . . . find Sara. I think she's looking for me. There's Kate. You guys should dance."

"And we will," Ben said easily. "But at the moment I was enjoying dancing with you."

"I enjoyed it, too." Jamie gave him a provocative look.

"Well, then, we should both do what we enjoy,

don't you think?" He held his arms out to her again.

"Maybe later," Jamie said, backing away from him. Then she fled to the kitchen.

What is going on? she thought, leaning her head against the cool refrigerator door. *All these guys— Jason, Scott, Ben. The guys my best friends like, and they're all coming on to me. It's like I've turned into some kind of a guy magnet.*

Admit it, you love it, a voice in her head said. *It's much more fun than being so tongue-tied you can't put together an intelligent sentence in the presence of a halfway cute guy. It's so much more fun to be on the inside looking out, than on the outside looking in.*

Wait. What's that?

Suddenly Jamie had the strangest sensation in the pit of her stomach. What was it? She knew she'd felt it before, but she couldn't think of where or when it had—

"Finyl Vinyl!" she exclaimed out loud. That was it. She'd had the same odd feeling when she'd met that girl, Callie.

Like I knew her. Like she was calling to me, somehow.

Without allowing herself to consider how crazy it seemed, Jamie quickly searched for Callie in the downstairs of Kate's huge house. Then she went back outside, into the backyard. She scrutinized all the faces in the pool. Nothing. Her skin felt hot, and kind of itchy. But the sensation was more mental than physical.

What is going on with me? I'm flirting with my friend's boyfriends. I meet some girl at the mall and feel like I've known her all my life even though I've never laid eyes on her before. This is so . . . so not me.

"Hormonal imbalance. Or harmonic convergence. Or my second house is in Mercury. Or something equally stupid," Jamie muttered. "Get over it. If you were still doing the 'zine, you wouldn't cover this because it would be too lame."

"Talking to yourself?"

A girl Jamie had never seen before had just walked up to her and posed the question.

"Sometimes I'm the only one who can stand my company," Jamie replied. But her heart was pounding.

This is just how it was with Callie. I have the same feeling about this girl, whoever she is.

"I'm Sue Lloyd," the girl said.

Sue Lloyd had a pretty, open face and deep, intelligent eyes. Eyes that, at the moment, were peering deeply into Jamie's.

"Jamie Dobrin. Do we know each other?"

Sue shrugged. "I feel like I know you from some-place. Maybe you came to dress rehearsal of the play I was supposed to be in? There was an audience, so—"

"What play was it?"

"It was called—"

Suddenly, out of nowhere, a lanky blond-haired guy materialized.

"Sue?"

"Hi, Billy," Sue said. "Billy Langley, this is Jamie

113

Dobrin. We're trying to figure out how we know each other."

Billy looked at Jamie. Something about the intensity of his gaze made her shiver. It wasn't a good shiver, either. "Maybe you just remind each other of other people," he suggested. "That happens all the time." It seemed to Jamie that he was telling them, more than posing a possibility.

"Oh, hey, Sue," Billy said, turning to Sue. "There's a phone call for you in the house."

"Who would call me here?" Sue wondered. "The only person who had the number is—"

"Your mom," Billy filled in quickly.

Sue rolled her eyes. "She's in overprotective mode again. Wait here," she told Jamie. "I'll be right back."

Billy smiled at Jamie as Sue headed off to the house, but the smile never seemed to reach those intense eyes of his.

"You have great eyes," she heard herself tell him. "Makes me wonder what you're thinking."

Oh, my gosh, I just said something flirtatious to a guy I disliked on sight.

What is going on, here?

Chapter 14

**** NATIONAL SECURITY MEMORANDUM #9 ****
EXTREME TOP SECRET, EYES-ONLY,
LIMITED DISTRIBUTION

THIS IS COPY NUMBER 7 OUT OF 15 TOTAL

From: Dr. Louise Warner, Chair, Substance Z project
To: Substance Z Recovery/Field Test Team
Re: Jamie Dobrin

Attached herewith are reports from two undercover field operatives who have infiltrated the lives of Substance Z subjects.

Undercover operative Paul Berman is going by the pseudonym Billy Langley. Operative Shannon Moore is going by the pseudonym Ann Smythe. Both are currently passing as high school students in the New Orleans area. "Billy" continues observation of Subject #3, Sue Lloyd, and has also met Jamie Dobrin, Subject #4. "Ann" made brief contact with Jamie Dobrin, at the New Orleans Centre mall.

That all our subjects seem to be somehow drawn to one another is of great concern. Thus far our field operatives have been successful at preventing in-depth communication between the subjects, but a decision is being taken as to whether this policy of diverting contact will or should continue.

After you have read the attached reports, DE-STROY THIS MEMO.

Chapter

15

Something was pounding inside Jamie's head. She really needed an aspirin, but she couldn't seem to move.

"I'll get it for you," Jason offered quickly.

"No, I will," Scott said.

Ben muscled both of them out of the way. "If Jamie needs an aspirin, then I'm the guy to—"

Pound-pound-pound.

"Jamie! Wake up!"

Jamie's eyes popped open. Cerise. Pounding on her door. Not inside her head at all. "What?" Jamie called groggily. She squinted bleary eyed at the clock on her nightstand. It was only 8:30 A.M. on Sunday. And Kate's party had lasted until really late the night before.

"Phone," Cerise barked. "I already said it about twenty times."

Jamie rolled over and picked up the phone. "Hello?"

"Jamie? 'Morning. It's Scott. I hope I didn't wake you."

"Uh . . ." Jamie was still too groggy to put together a gracious reply.

"Sorry, it sounds like I did," Scott said. "I'm one of those insane morning people. And it's so gorgeous out, I just got this idea of going out to the LaGrange Bayou for the day. You know, a picnic. Interested?"

Jamie shook the fog from her head. Scott was on the phone. He had just invited her to spend the day with him at the bayou. Which, yes, was used for picnics and Frisbee-throwing and general frolicking during the day, but was *the* make-out spot at night.

"Are a whole group of kids going or something?" Jamie asked carefully.

"A big group. Two," Scott said. "You and me. That a problem?"

"Kinda." Jamie sat up. "What about Lisa?"

"We're not really a couple or anything."

"She thinks you are," Jamie said.

"Well, I can't help what she thinks. So, you up for it?"

"I have to admit, Scott, I'm really, really tempted," Jamie said, almost purring into the phone. "But Lisa is one of my best friends. So even if you don't think you're a couple, I couldn't do that to her."

"Well, if you change your mind—"

"Sure," Jamie said. "And believe me, Scott, I'll be thinking about you."

Jamie hung up.

"Believe me, Scott, I'll be thinking about you?" Did I really just say that? Jamie shuddered at her own words. *The girl who said that is no one I know,* she thought, getting out of bed. *Although it was kinda fun.*

She knew she'd never be able to fall back to sleep now, so she decided to take a shower and start the day. When she came out of the bathroom, towel-drying her hair, the phone was ringing. She hurried over to it so Cerise wouldn't scream at her again.

"Hello?"

"Jamie? Hi. It's Will Jacobs. I'm in your English class?"

"Right." Jamie sat on the edge of her bed. Why was Will Jacobs calling her? He was very good-looking, and vice president of the sophomore class, but as far as Jamie knew, he was dating Patsi Ponder, the head JV cheerleader.

"I heard Kate's party last night was the bomb," Will went on. "I had to go to a thing with my parents at the country club or I would have been there."

"Too bad you weren't there," Jamie said. "I saved a slow dance for you."

Her hand flew to her mouth, as if she could keep herself from saying anything else that provocative.

"Yeah?" Will asked, his voice growing more intimate. "I would have liked that."

"Me, too."

I did it again. It just popped out!

"I mean, as a friend," she amended lamely.

"I don't know," Will teased, "it sounded like you meant more than that. Did you know that Patsi and I broke up?"

"No. I'm sorry."

"She's dating some guy named Marley Wilson who goes to Overton," Will said. "He's some kinda reggae freak, something like that."

"Hard to picture Patsi with a reggae freak."

"Who knows, maybe opposites attract. Anyway, I was wondering if you'd like to go to that new coffeehouse on Bouvier Street tonight? The house band is supposed to rock."

Will Jacobs had just asked her out. She couldn't be more shocked if he had shown up at her front door in pearls and an evening gown. *Will is so cool and so popular. Not to mention filthy rich.* Jamie felt a thrill of excitement.

"That might be fun," Jamie said casually. "Who's going?"

"Well, I just got my license, finally, so I'm driving," Will said. "I'll see who else is up for it. Sound cool?"

"Sure, country club boy," Jamie teased. "Call me later and give me details, okay?"

"You got it. And, Jamie?"

"Hmmm?"

"Wear that great perfume you've been wearing to school lately, okay? See ya."

Jamie jumped off her bed and twirled around her room. She had a date. With a really hot guy.

A guy who you've never had a single conversation with before, she reminded herself. *A guy who you and your buds always thought was kind of a snob. A guy who is mean to kids he doesn't consider cool enough.*

"But he's hot," Jamie told her reflection in the mirror. "And, anyway, maybe I was all wrong about him." She held her hair off her neck. Maybe she'd wear it up tonight. She smiled at her reflection. Will wanted her to wear the same "great" perfume. Only she hadn't been wearing any perfume at all.

And I'm just going to have to make sure he gets close enough to find out for himself.

By noon six guys had called Jamie and asked her out. She made a list and ranked them according to how cute they were and how interested she was in them. Of course, none of these guys was Nick. Funny how it seemed like the more popular she got with other guys, the less popular she got with him.

She really needed to talk this over with Sara, so she quickly punched Sara's phone number into her phone.

"Torres residence, this is Sara speaking," she answered.

"You're gonna be away at college and you'll probably still answer the phone like that out of habit," Jamie teased.

"It's how my parents trained us to answer the phone," Sara said stiffly. "You know that."

"I was joking, Sar. Have fun last night?"

"Sure." Sara's voice sounded odd. Distant. Kind of cold.

"What's wrong?"

"Nothing."

"Come on, this is *me* you're talking to. Did another brother or sister drop out of school or something? Because you are acting very strange."

"I'm not the one acting strange, Jamie."

"What are you talking about? I've hardly even talked to you since the kite thing. I kept looking for you at Kate's party last night—"

"I left early," Sara said.

"Well, why didn't you tell me?" Jamie exclaimed.

"I would have had to fight my way through the crowd of guys around you to do it," Sara said pointedly.

Jamie laughed. "Come on, Sar, you have to admit, this is kind of fantastic. It's like all of a sudden I got super popular. I know exactly what to say to guys all the time."

"But who's saying it?" Sara asked.

"What are you talking about?"

"I'm talking about you, Jamie. Why are you—"

Jamie's call-waiting beeped. "Hold on a sec, Sara. I'll be right back."

She put Sara's call on hold and clicked in the other one. "Hello?"

"Jamie, Jamie, Jamie."

She recognized Ben's deep, sexy, self-confident voice. Now, Ben was hot. Probably the hottest guy in their entire school. Before Kate, he'd been dating a girl Cerise knew from college.

Ben Rogers was calling *her*.

"Ben, Ben, Ben," she teased.

"Did I mention how great you looked last night?" he asked her.

"I don't know. So many people told me that, it's hard to remember."

He laughed. "You're a brat, you know that?"

"Thank you. I'll take that as a compliment."

"You know, we never did get to finish that dance last night," he reminded her.

"Oh, really?" Jamie lay down on her bed, smiling up at the ceiling. "I honestly can't remember."

"You're bad," he scolded. "Which is quite intriguing."

"Is it?" she purred.

"Actually, I dreamt about you last night," he confided. "I thought maybe we could get together and I could tell you all about it."

"Tell, or show-and-tell?" Jamie asked.

"That'll be your call," Ben said. "But I should warn you. I can be very persuasive. So, let's set a date."

"What a good—"

Date. Which rhymed with Kate.

As in: Ben is Kate's boyfriend. What are you doing, Jamie? Kate's into Ben just as much as Sara is into—

Oh, no. Sara.

"Ben? I have to go," she said quickly.

"But—"

Jamie clicked into her other call, where Sara had been on hold forever. Only Sara was no longer there.

Jamie paced across her bedroom, just as she'd done for the past hour. It was one o'clock in the afternoon. Kate had called her just after she'd hung up with Sara, to say that she and Lisa and Sara were coming over because they needed to talk with her. Jamie had a feeling it wasn't going to be about anything good.

"Jam?" Sara called upstairs. "We're here."

"Come on up," she called down.

Stay calm, Jamie told herself. *These are your friends. Okay, so you forgot about Sara's being on the other line. You called her right back and left a message apologizing. Anyone can make a mistake.*

Kate, Lisa, and Sara trooped into Jamie's room. None of them was smiling. "Gee, happy happy happy campers," Jamie quipped, trying to hide her nervousness. "What's up?"

Kate stood in the doorway, Sara on one side of her, Lisa on the other. Kate folded her arms. "Jamie Dobrin, this is an intervention."

"A *what?*" Jamie sat on her bed, totally confused.

"When addicts are out of control, sometimes people who care about them confront them with how their behavior is ruining everyone's lives," Kate said. "And now we're confronting you."

"Which might make sense if I was addicted to something," Jamie said. "But I don't smoke, drink, or do drugs, so—"

"There are other things a person can become addicted to," Sara said.

Lisa nodded. "Such as guys."

Jamie shook her head. "Guys? You think I'm addicted to guys? You three? Now, that's ridiculous. Take a look in the mirror!"

"No, it isn't," Sara said. "You have turned into a completely different Jamie than the Jamie we know. You flirt with every guy who comes near you. No guy in the world is safe."

"And no girl's boyfriend is safe, either," Lisa added, her voice tinged with hurt.

"You have it all wrong," Jamie said. "First of all, how can I be addicted to guys when I have never gone out on an actual date with one? And second of all, I would never, ever go out with one of your boyfriends. I thought you knew me better than that."

Sara slid her back down the wall and sat on the carpet. "We used to know you, Jamie. But we don't know you anymore."

"Because the you you've become isn't someone we like," Kate said.

Tears sprang to Jamie's eyes. "That is so unfair.

Who was it who quit *American Grrls* just because they got interested in guys? It wasn't me."

"Maybe we just outgrew the 'zine," Lisa said.

"Well, then, maybe I just outgrew the three of you," Jamie snapped, so angry and hurt she could barely speak to them at all.

There was a long moment of silence.

"You don't mean that, Jamie," Sara finally said. "I know you don't."

"Okay, maybe I don't," Jamie allowed. "But this—this intervention thing is total bull. Reality check: I'm the only one of the four of us who doesn't have a boyfriend, remember?"

"It's not about that," Kate said.

"Oh, well, then, Kate, since you know everything, why don't you explain it to me?" Jamie jeered.

"All right, I will," Kate said. "You flirted with Jason and with Scott and with Ben. You can't even have a conversation with a guy anymore unless you're flirting with him. Do you deny that?"

"Maybe I did get better at talking with guys—"

"No, you didn't," Kate interrupted. "You got better at putting on this whole fake, flirty front with them. It's a big joke."

"Right," Lisa agreed. "You don't really get to know them and they don't know you."

"They're just responding to the vibe you're putting out," Kate said. "So don't flatter yourself."

Jamie's eyes narrowed. "You're wrong. Because here's what I think: I think you're all just jealous because your boyfriends keep asking me out. The truth hurts, doesn't it?"

"Let's see what the truth is, Jamie," Kate said. "Choose or Lose."

Jamie sighed. "Choose or lose what?"

Kate, Lisa, and Sara all looked at one another, then nodded almost imperceptibly. "Okay, here it is," Kate said. "Jamie, would you choose to prove to us that you can not talk about guys, flirt with guys, or be with guys, by going guy-free for the next twenty-four hours?"

"And we'll be with you to make sure," Lisa added.

"Or what?" Jamie asked.

"Or lose," Sara said. "Lose us. As your friends. Forever."

Chapter

16

Seven o'clock at night.

Six hours since Jamie's friends had begun their intervention. To Jamie, it seemed more like six hundred hours.

First, her friends had stayed with her in shifts, one after the other. Jamie had mostly ignored whichever of them was with her. She read, or did homework, or watched TV. She was too hurt and angry to engage them in conversation. And they didn't seem to expect her to talk to them, anyway.

What they didn't know was this: The no-guy thing was driving her crazy.

She picked up *The Heart Is a Lonely Hunter*. But *heart* made her think of her Loverock. Which made her think about falling in love. Which of course made her think about guys.

She clicked on the TV. An old episode of *The Real World*. One of the guys looked a lot like Jason. It had been so much fun flirting with Jason, when they were flying their kites together. Jason had given her that little-boy look, and—

No. Off-limits thinking. Homework, then. Geometry. She opened her textbook. A note fell out.

"Do you like Nick Brooks?"

She slammed the book shut.

Even though her friends—more like former friends and current jail keepers—couldn't know what she was thinking, she wanted to prove to herself that they were wrong. She was not obsessed with guys and flirting. No way. In fact, if anyone was obsessed with guys, it was the three of them.

She began to drum her fingers on her desk, just for something to do. "Would you please stop that?" Sara asked from Jamie's bed. "I'm trying to study."

"Sure. Who cares if it's *my room* at *my house*?"

"Irritable," Sara observed. "But then, all addicts are irritable when they're going through withdrawal."

"Would you stop saying that?" Jamie demanded. "I am not going through—"

"Withdrawal," Kate said from the doorway. Lisa was standing next to her. They were both carrying their overnight bags.

"Gee, a PJ party," Jamie said sarcastically. "I'll go

make some popcorn and we can play Choose or Lose."

"No, we can't," Lisa said, bouncing down on the bed. "That game always ends up being about you-know-whos."

"That's right," Jamie agreed. "Let's go to the videotape. Which one of us was the only one who never wanted to play that game?"

"You," Sara allowed. "But you've changed, Jamie. You know you have."

"Okay, maybe I have. But so have you. All three of you. Why am I the only one who was supposed to stay the same?" Jamie asked.

Silence. No one answered her question.

Because they know I'm telling the truth, Jamie thought self-righteously. *I'm right and they're wrong.*

"We've all changed," Lisa said hesitantly. "It's more than that." She looked over at Kate, hoping Kate could explain it better than she could.

"We're teenage girls. Being into guys is a normal part of life," Kate said.

"Then why are you guys treating me like some kind of leper when I'm the very last of the four of us to get into guys?" Jamie asked, truly perplexed.

"Liking guys is one thing, Jamie," Kate replied. "You are something else."

"Ask yourself this, Jamie," Sara said. "You like Nick, right? Even though, as far as I know, he's the only guy who hasn't fallen for your flirting."

"*Cheap* flirting," Kate corrected.

"Oh, thanks—" Jamie began.

"Ask yourself this, Jam," Sara went on earnestly. "Would I, your bud Sara, ever flirt with Nick? Would Lisa? Would Kate?"

"Maybe not," Jamie muttered.

"Definitely not and you know it," Kate said. "It's like you're in some kind of contest to see how many guys you can get to like you—"

"And then when they do start to like you, you claim that you weren't really flirting, you were just talking to them," Lisa added.

"You guys are blowing this totally out of—"

"Hey, I hate to break into this Marcia Brady moment," Cerise said from the doorway, "but there's a guy here for you, Jam."

Four sets of eyes stared accusingly at Jamie.

"I have no idea who it is," Jamie said.

"His name's Will something or other," Cerise added. "He says you guys have a date."

Heat flooded Jamie's face. Will Jacobs. *Oh, no.*

"B-but I didn't make a date with him," Jamie protested. "I mean, not a definite one. He was supposed to call me—"

"Tell him, not me." Cerise disappeared down the hall.

"Congratulations, Jamie," Kate said icily. "You managed to make it"—she checked her watch—"six hours and twenty-two minutes without a guy."

"But you still flunk," Lisa said.

Jamie looked from face to face to face. "You three would really stop being friends with me? Really?"

"It's one thing to start liking boys, Jamie," Sara said. "But you've turned into a completely different person. Someone the old Jamie wouldn't have liked."

"Okay," she said. "Do whatever you want." She headed for the door.

"Are you going out with him?" Kate asked.

Jamie turned back to them. "First, I'm going to tell Will I'm not going out with him. Second, Choose or Lose. What would you rather do? Have an honest talk like we haven't had in years—and you guys have to do as much listening as you do talking—or give up on five years of friendship?" Jamie turned on her heel and walked out.

Jamie plucked nervously at her cuticles. They were a mess. She and her friends had been talking for two hours, saying a lot of things that they'd held inside for a long time.

"We were wrong to just drop out of the 'zine like we did," Kate admitted.

"It was so horrible for me," Jamie lamented. "Like all of you were deserting me. For guys."

"But the 'zine wasn't a . . . a marriage," Lisa told her.

"Maybe, in a way, it was," Sara said thoughtfully. "And then, one by one, we kind of cheated on Jamie. And like she said, we deserted her. All because we started getting so guy-obsessed ourselves."

Sara's eyes met Jamie's. "I'm sorry, Jam. I really am. I never looked at it that way before."

"To tell you the truth, I didn't, either," Kate admitted, pushing some hair behind her ear.

"Remember when we said we would never, ever put guys before our own interests, or dreams, or before our friendship with each other?" Jamie asked them wistfully.

"But all girls do that when—" Lisa began.

"No," Sara said firmly. "All girls don't do that. And even if they did, we're not 'all girls.' We don't do that. Not anymore. Agreed?"

"Agreed," Kate said.

"Agreed," from Lisa.

"Definitely agreed," Jamie said fervently. "And how about if next Friday we all meet here, order pizzas like we used to, and figure out if we're going to end *American Grrls*, or keep it going and change it, or what?"

They all agreed. Then they hugged one another, just like they used to. It was so great that they all began laughing at once. The phone rang.

"If it's a guy, she's in Peru somewhere," Lisa ordered.

Jamie laughed and reached for the phone. "Hello?"

"Hi, Jamie?"

"Yes?"

"This is Billy Langley. I don't know if you remember me. I'm a friend of Sue Lloyd's. We met at your friend Kate's party after the football game."

"Oh, sure I remember you, Billy," Jamie said.

Her friends were all staring at her. But what was she supposed to do, hang up on him just because he was male? That would be ridiculous.

"I called to invite you to a party," Bill went on. "Next Friday."

"Um, a party? Next Friday?" Jamie repeated, stalling for time.

Why don't I just say "no"? she wondered. *I got a creepy feeling from him. I didn't like his eyes. I don't owe him anything. So why don't I just say no?*

She could not get the word *no* out of her mouth.

"This might sound like some big line," Billy went on, "and I know we hardly talked at all at that party, but I'd really like a chance to get to know you better."

"I'd like to get to know you better, too," Jamie said. "Your eyes are really intense and—"

Oh, my gosh. What am I doing? I can't go out with him on Friday. I just made plans with my friends.

Jamie looked over at her friends' angry, hurt faces. "I have to go, Billy," she whispered, and hung up the phone.

"Why?" Sara asked. "I just want to know why, Jamie?"

"I don't know! I don't even like him, but I couldn't help myself. It was like I was outside of myself, watching this idiotic girl flirt with a guy she doesn't even like, just to prove that she can get him."

"Exactly," Kate said, her voice flat.

"But that wasn't me," Jamie protested. "I mean, that isn't me."

"I don't know who you are anymore," Sara said.

As if by unspoken agreement, Sara, Kate, and Lisa gathered up their things. "Intervention is over. Maybe you need some time alone," Sara said.

"Just you and whatever guy was at the other end of that phone," Kate added.

"I'm sorry, really—"

Sara shook her head. " 'Sorry' is not enough anymore, Jamie."

Jamie was more miserable than she could ever remember. She'd lost her three best friends in the world. It was her own fault.

She'd called Kate and Lisa once each, and Sara three times, but only got their answering machines. She left messages of apology, because she didn't know what else to do. She got up, wandered over to the window, and gazed up at the night sky, trying to understand how everything had gotten so messed up.

The really funny thing is, I was happier back when I was tongue-tied around boys, she thought. *At least I had Matt as an e-mail pal. I've barely written to him, lately, even though he's probably the only pal I have left.*

Being a flirt wasn't the real her, she knew that now. It was one thing to be natural around boys, to get to know them.

But all that fake come-on stuff actually just keeps them from knowing the real you, she realized.

It was as if a lightbulb had just gone on in her brain. Flirting with every single guy was just as much a way of hiding as being shy was.

"Too bad my psychological breakthrough came a little too late," she said to herself. She rested her forehead on the cool glass of her window and sighed.

What was done can be undone.

Jamie looked around. Had someone just spoken to her?

What was done can be undone.

"Okay, this is officially bizarre."

Because she felt as if the voice was coming from inside her. What's more, she understood what the voice meant. She went to her nightstand and picked up the Loverock.

Suddenly she knew that if she slept with the Loverock under her pillow, she could go back to being the girl she used to be.

Somehow, she knew this was a one-time offer. Or she'd remain an out-of-control flirt forever. That thought made her shudder. Her friends were right. She didn't like the girl she had become.

Jamie stuck the Loverock under her pillow and crawled into bed. Her last thoughts before she fell asleep were: *Please let me learn how to be my real self.*

And please let me find a way to get my friends back.

Chapter

17

❦

Jamie awoke to a bird singing outside her window. As she lay in bed, listening to it, she heard words in its song. *It's a new dawn, Jamie. You can make it whatever you want it to be.*

The song suddenly stopped, and with a rush of wings, the bird flew away.

Right, Jamie thought sourly. *That's what really happens with lovely Hallmark-card moments. Reality is a little different.*

She'd rolled over and felt the Loverock, hard under her pillow. And, as it dug into the back of her head, the events of the day before—the two weeks before, really—came flooding back at her.

She had turned into the kind of girl who put

guys before her friends. Because of that, she'd lost their friendship.

Unless . . .

Jamie reached under her pillow for the Loverock. Had sleeping with the rock under her pillow worked? Had she been able to change herself back into the girl she once was, and wanted to be again?

She sat up, holding the Loverock in her right palm. It glittered as magically as it had the first time she looked at it. "Are you really magical?" she whispered. "Or is this all just some stupid, juvenile fantasy I invented?" Her hand grew warmer and little vibrations traveled up her arm.

My imagination, she told herself. *No one else feels that. And what difference does it make, anyway? I have to take control of my own life.*

Filled with energy and purpose, she got out of bed. *What's done can be undone. But I can't erase the past, no matter what,* Jamie realized. *And I can't make my friends like me again. I suppose the only person I can change, really, is myself.*

She quickly showered and dressed for school. Then she loaded her backpack with her schoolbooks and looped one arm through it. The glittering Loverock caught her eye. Impetuously she picked it up and threw it into her backpack, too.

Maybe it'll bring me good luck, Jamie thought as she scribbled a note to let her parents know she was biking over to school early. *Right about now I'll take all the good luck I can get.*

Jamie had thought that arriving early at school would get the day started right, with a new attitude. But still, as she trudged up the walk to the high school, her heart began that old tap-dance thing. Even with her newly found so-called maturity and insight, she had no idea what would happen, whether she could stop being, as Kate put it, "a cheap flirt."

But one thing was certain: The only hope she had of getting her friends back was to stop. She had wished for it with all her might and had slept on the Loverock. Now she would find out if she'd changed.

Jamie decided to head for the library. Maybe she could distract herself from her life with a book about someone else's. In the library, she told herself, she would be less likely to run into Sara, Lisa, and Kate. Because, frankly, she was afraid to face them.

She had just reached the doors of the library when someone called to her. "Hey, Jamie!"

She turned around. Jason's friend Shawn, whom she'd met at the kite festival, was hurrying over to her.

"Hi," she said, surprised to see him. "Wait, don't you go to Overton?"

"Good call. The Louisiana high school debate teams are arguing gun control this year. And sectionals are here, this morning."

"I didn't even know there was such a thing," Jamie admitted.

"Oh, yeah. It's big. Lots of future lawyers. Also kids who just love to hear the sound of their own voice."

"So, which are you?" Jamie asked.

"Probably both," Shawn admitted.

"Well, I like to hear the sound of your voice, too." Jamie smiled at him, gazing up at him from under her eyelashes. "Did anyone ever tell you how cute your—"

She stopped speaking. Her eyes grew huge. She backed away from him. "What? What's wrong?" Shawn asked.

All Jamie could do was shake her head.

"Are you sick or something?" He moved swiftly toward her, holding a hand up to her forehead.

"No, don't!"

His hand flew off her, as if she'd burnt him.

"I . . . I have to go." Jamie fled blindly, no destination in mind, no idea where to go, hot tears obscuring her vision. She knew the truth now. And the truth was the thing she had feared the most. She had flirted shamelessly with the very first guy she saw. Not because she liked him. But because she hadn't been able to help herself.

The school hallways were beginning to fill up. Ahead, a group of girls was walking toward her— girls Jamie knew. The last thing she wanted was to have to deal with them, so she turned right and headed into the auditorium.

The vast hall was dark and empty, like something from a horror movie. Except everyone knew that stuff was make-believe, so being scared at horror movies was half the fun. But Jamie's fears came from real life.

This kind of scared isn't fun at all, she ruminated.

Not sure where to go, she walked down the center aisle to the stage, climbed the stairs onto the stage, and then wended her way toward the green room. Formerly a large supply closet, it had been painted green last year and converted into a backstage lounge for student actors. Right now it was deserted. Which was perfect.

Jamie desperately wanted a place where she could cry in private. She threw herself onto the old tweed couch and sobbed her heart out. The truth was clear. Nothing had changed. She still couldn't stop herself from flirting.

The more she thought about how her life would be without her three best friends—especially Sara—the harder she cried. She didn't want to make friends with the kind of girls who would befriend her now—girls with nothing but guys on their mind.

Even if Kate and Lisa and Sara do get a little boy-crazy, they still care about other things, too, Jamie thought. *Sara still does volunteer work; Kate plays volleyball; Lisa's in the school play.*

What they don't care about anymore, what they'll never care about again, is me.

That thought made her miserable.

Tears choked her.

"Jamie?"

She looked up. Nick Brooks stood in the door-way.

"I was in the scene shop working on scenery for the play, and I thought I heard someone crying."

Nick. And her. Here.

Now the nightmare that was her life was officially complete.

Chapter

18

"*N*ick, please, go away." Jamie buried her face in her hands.

He didn't. Instead he came into the green room, turned on one of the floor lamps, and sat next to her on the couch. There were some napkins from a fast-food restaurant on the scarred coffee table. Wordlessly he handed them to her. She wiped her eyes and blew her nose. Not that it did any good.

"Well, now everything is officially perfect," Jamie said, shuddering back the last of her sobs. "I've lost my friends forever. And you, of all people, find me back here like this."

"I didn't mean to intrude—"

"See? I can't do anything right. I just made you

feel terrible when it isn't you at all. It's me. It's everything. My entire life."

He looked confused. "I don't understand."

"Of course you don't. Because I'm an inarticulate, sopping wet mess who *still* flirts with every guy in sight."

He scratched his chin. "You're upset because you're inarticulate? Or because you're a flirt?"

"I used to be so shy and tongue-tied around boys." Jamie stared down at the used paper napkin, rolling tiny bits of it between her fingers. "All my friends had boyfriends, but I couldn't even carry on a conversation with a guy. In my mind I knew what I wanted to say, but I just couldn't ever get the words to come out right."

"So you'd clam up?" Nick asked.

Jamie nodded. "You can't imagine how horrible it was. The more you clam up, the worse it gets. It's like shyness feeds on itself. Then my friends all stopped writing our 'zine, because they got so into guys—"

"*American Grrls,*" Nick filled in.

Jamie was surprised. "How do you know that?"

"I used to read it," he admitted. "I thought it was great, too. I could never understand why it ended."

"Well, now you know. I tried to do it all myself, but I couldn't. So then I thought, if only I could learn to be sexy and flirty around guys like my friends were, everything would be okay again, and I'd even get the guy I'm crazy about to—"

Jamie stopped. She closed her eyes. No. This could not be happening. She was pouring out her heart about loving Nick. *To* Nick.

"Some guy you're crazy about?" he prompted.

"I don't suppose you could pretend you never heard me say that, could you?" Jamie asked meekly.

"If you're concerned that I'd tell him, don't be. I can keep a secret."

Jamie searched his face for any sign that he was teasing her, but none was there. Was it really possible that he didn't know she was talking about him?

"I know this is going to sound incredibly lame," Jamie began. She looked at the wall, the floor, every place except into his eyes. Because that would just hurt too much. "I made this wish that I could talk to guys. And, you know, flirt with them. Like my friends."

Nick nodded, waiting.

"So . . . this is the part that's even more lame—it happened. Suddenly I could flirt with every guy. And I got all this attention from them. It was so much fun."

"Was it?"

"Yeah," she admitted. "Which probably makes me sound incredibly shallow—"

"I don't think so," Nick assured her. "I mean, not unless it became, like, the focus of your life, or something."

He seemed to be studying her carefully. Jamie knew how awful the truth would sound, but for some reason, she wanted to tell him the truth, anyway.

"It did," Jamie admitted. "I couldn't turn it off. And I still can't. Which is why my friends have dropped me and I don't blame them. And on top of that, the guy I like is still clueless."

Nick put his sneakers up on the edge of the coffee table. "Well, I'm not gonna do one of those things where I offer to ask the guy if he likes you and then come back and tell you."

"I wouldn't want you to," Jamie said quickly.

Nick looked at her sideways. "That is, if I even know him."

"You know him."

Silence. Nick was waiting for her to say who she had a crush on. Big joke. Jamie stared so hard at the pile of napkins that they blurred before her eyes. She couldn't tell him. She just couldn't.

"You know what's really funny?" she finally said. "The guy I like so much . . . he doesn't know me."

Nick made a noise of disgust under his breath. "One of those famous-guy crushes? James Van Der Beek? Scott Speedman, Freddie—?"

"I'm not that pathetic." She managed a small laugh. "I mean . . . I never let this guy get to know me. Never let him see the real me."

"Oh. Well, that's different, then. How come?"

Jamie shrugged. "I guess because I was afraid if

he knew me, he wouldn't really like me. I was scared."

Nick sat back on the couch. "I can understand that."

"You can?"

He nodded. "What's funny is, there's this girl I've liked for a really long time. The difference is, I knew this girl really well."

Jamie's heart fell. Nick liked someone else. That was the reason he'd never shown any interest in her. *It must be that cute girl he was dancing with after I burped in his face,* Jamie thought. *Which means I went through everything I went through for nothing. Because there was never a chance of getting Nick to like me.*

"So," Jamie began, her voice small, "since you know this girl so well, are the two of you to-gether?"

"It's complicated," Nick replied.

"Well, *that* I understand." She reached for another napkin and blew her nose again. "I must look like death warmed over. Some girls look pretty when they cry. I get red-faced and swollen and gunky."

Nick laughed. "I think 'crying pretty' only happens to Julia Roberts."

Jamie managed a weak smile. "You want to hear the funniest part of all? I have this friend in Wisconsin, named Matt. We've been e-mail pals for a long time. And even back when I was so shy around guys I couldn't put two words together, I could be my real self with him online."

"Weird," Nick agreed. "How come?"

Jamie thought a moment. "I guess we could be completely honest with each other because we lived so far apart. So there was no fear of rejection or anything. I mean, the closest I'm ever gonna get to seeing him is the photo he sent me."

"And the photo you sent him."

"Yeah." She got up to throw her used napkins into the trash. "A picture from last year. Which wasn't exactly the best—"

She stopped. Because Nick was standing there. Holding her picture. The one she'd sent to Matt. "It's decent," he said, studying the photo.

"Where did you get that?"

"You sent it to me." He put it back in his wallet.

"Wait." Jamie clapped one palm to her forehead. "Oh, this is crazy. You can't be—"

"14 ZZZDreamer. Yeah, I can."

"B-but Matt lives in LaCrosse, Wisconsin! And he has blond hair and wears an earring in one ear and—"

"My bud," Nick confessed. "I sent you his picture. And I lived in LaCrosse until I was nine."

Jamie felt dizzy. She had to sit down. Nick sat, too. "Why?" she asked, bewildered and hurt. "Why would you do that to me?"

"I didn't mean to do anything to you, Jamie. It's just that . . . well, I guess it's true confession time." Nick inhaled deeply and blew the air out. "Last year, when we started e-mailing each other, the truth is, I was petrified of even talking to you at school."

"*You* were scared of *me?*" Jamie asked incredulously.

"Yeah. So I gave myself a different name online. And sent you someone else's picture."

"But why? I am utterly lost, here."

"Because online, hiding behind Matt, I could totally be myself with you," Nick confessed.

"But you never even talked to me!" Jamie protested. "And when I turned into this great flirt, you were the only guy who still wouldn't give me the time of day."

"Because that great flirt wasn't the real Jamie. The Jamie I knew. And loved."

Her mouth fell open. "You—?"

He looked away from her. "And I was afraid I'd lost the real Jamie forever."

"No," she whispered, reaching for his hand. "I'm right here."

He turned back to her, his gorgeous, deep-set eyes meeting hers. "And I was afraid I'd never get to do this." He leaned over and gave her the softest kiss in the world.

Jamie's eyes glistened with happiness. "I can't believe this is really happening."

Nick laughed. "I feel kinda like I'm dreaming, too." He softly kissed her again.

"You know, you have a lot of lost time to make

up for," Jamie said softly. "You should probably do that one more time."

This time he put his arms around her. And kissed her so that the whole world fell away, and there was nothing but her, and Nick, and this moment . . .

"Whoa, walked in on the old mack session."

Jamie gently pulled away from Nick and opened her eyes. Drake. Gorgeous senior Drake. The hottest of the hot Drake.

"Looks like you're good at that, Jamie," Drake added with a knowing grin. Jamie looked thoughtful for a moment. And she realized that what she felt for Drake was . . . nothing. She had absolutely no desire to flirt with him.

None. None at all!

She looked at Nick. "I'm only good at it with someone I really care about," she said, so happy that it was finally true.

"Guess that lets me out," Drake said cheerfully. "Carry on, you two."

Nick grinned. "Well, you heard him. Carry on."

And they did.

After school Jamie practically floated home to her bedroom.

If I'm dreaming, I never want to wake up, she thought. *Nick loves me. And I love him.*

She dropped her backpack on her desk, knocking over a framed photo. She picked it up. It was a photo of her with Sara, Lisa, and Kate when they were kids, at the beach. They all had their arms around one another. Jamie was wearing Kate's infamous bikini.

Instantly Jamie's good mood disappeared. All day at school she had avoided Sara, Lisa, and Kate, and, as far as Jamie could tell, they had avoided her, too. Even in the cafeteria at lunch. Jamie had eaten alone. Something in the very center of her felt hollow. And as much as she loved Nick, it wasn't a place he could fill.

She missed her friends. So much. She pulled the Loverock out of her backpack. "No matter how magic you are, I guess you can't bring my friends back to me," she said.

Strange. The Loverock wasn't vibrating in her hand as it used to. Maybe that really had just been her imagination.

"Choose or Lose," Jamie said to herself. "Choose or Lose. And I lost. Unless . . ."

An idea flew into her mind. And refused to fly out again. The only question was, could it work? She put the Loverock back on her nightstand, grabbed her backpack and the photo she'd knocked over, and bolted out of her room and out the front door.

"Why, Jamie, what a nice surprise!" Mrs. Torres said when she answered the doorbell. "We haven't seen you here in a long time."

"I know," Jamie told Sara's mom. "I'm sorry. I've missed you. Is Sara around?"

"Upstairs, studying," Mrs. Torres told Jamie. "Which is exactly what you should be doing," she added, and it was clear she was only half-joking.

Normally, Jamie would have smiled at Mrs. Torres's fixation on academics. But she was too wrought up inside. *What if Sara thinks this is completely stupid? What if she totally rejects me? It could happen.*

"But I'll make an exception for you, since this is a day of the week that ends in the letter *y.*" Mrs. Torres winked. "Go on upstairs. She's in her room."

Jamie thanked her and headed for Sara's room. She'd been in the Torreses' home many, many times. But today it felt different. Distant. Foreign. Scary, in a way.

What if she tells me to get lost?

Seconds later Jamie was knocking on Sara's door. "Mom, can you please not come in now, I'm doing math and it's very hard," Sara called.

Jamie pushed the door open. Sara looked up. Her eyes locked with Jamie's.

"Hi," Jamie said softly.

"Hi." Sara's voice was noncommittal. "This is a surprise."

"I had to talk to you. Can I come in?"

"Only if you promise not to steal my boyfriend," Sara replied, folding her arms. "But with you I know that's pretty much impossible."

Jamie winced at that, but she knew she deserved it. "Ten minutes," she promised. "Just hear me out. Please. Isn't our friendship worth it?"

"I already heard you out. So did Kate and Lisa. And it didn't work. So I don't see why—"

Jamie reached into her backpack and took out the photo of the four friends at the beach. Wordlessly she handed it to Sara. Sara studied the photo and her eyes misted over.

"I wanted you to have this," Jamie told her, "whether you wanted to listen to me or not. I knew this might happen, that you might not want to listen to me. So please. Keep it. To remind you of how great we all were together, a long time ago. Okay?"

"Thanks," Sara responded, her voice husky. "This means a lot to me."

"Okay, then, see ya." Jamie hitched up her backpack and headed for the door.

Four words stopped her.

"Where are you going?" Sara asked.

Jamie didn't turn around. "Home."

"No," Sara said. "Talk to me. It can't hurt to hear what you have to say."

Jamie came back and sat on the edge of Sara's bed. Then she poured her heart out to her former best friend. About their friendship. Their hopes and their dreams. And about how she was pretty sure she wasn't guy-crazy anymore. About how much they would all lose by losing each other.

When Jamie was done, Sara still appeared to be skeptical. "I'd love to believe you," Sara said. "I *want* to believe you. But you said just the same thing the other night, when we were all over at your house. And then look what happened."

"That was different," Jamie defended herself.

"Different from what?"

Jamie sagged. It was no use. She wasn't going to convince Sara that she had changed. The whole idea was ridiculous. She should never have come over. She should have stayed home. Gone on the computer. Chatted with her online friends. Called Nick.

No, a voice inside her said. *You can't give up when you've come this far. You can do better.*

Choose or Lose.

"That's it," Jamie said aloud.

"What's it?"

"Choose or Lose, Choose or Lose. Of course."

Sara looked confused. "Is that supposed to make sense?"

Jamie sprang up from the bed. "You asked what's different now. I'll tell you what's different. We're going to play Choose or Lose. Two rounds. You and me and Kate and Lisa. But you have to promise that if I win, we'll all be friends again. If I lose, you have every right to hate me and off our friendship forever."

"Well, I don't know why you'd want to be friends with girls who don't want to be friends with you," Sara said. "Besides, I have no idea what you're talking about."

But then Jamie told her. And as she explained

her idea, Sara's expression went from very skeptical to neutral to an approving nod. "Two rounds of Choose or Lose, under your new rules," Sara repeated. "Okay, I'm in. And I bet Kate and Lisa will be, too, after I talk to them. But I'm telling you, Jamie. If you lose it's over. Really over. No more chances." Their eyes locked once again.

"You didn't used to be this tough," Jamie observed.

"I didn't used to get double-crossed by my former best friend," Sara explained.

Their eyes met again. And it was perfectly clear. This was Jamie's last chance.

Chapter

19

❦

*S*aturday night. The night Jamie had chosen for Choose or Lose.

Jamie was dressed for a party, in a slinky black skirt and a snug little pink-and-black top. Her hair was up, with tendrils hanging down, and she wore a thin, beaded choker around her neck.

Bruce Woodson, a junior on the football team, was having a big bash to celebrate the team's win the night before. Mostly juniors and seniors would be there, but Jamie, with her newfound popularity, had easily gotten her and her former friends invited.

Former friends. She found it so hard to think of them that way.

Jamie had walked to Bruce's; Sara and Lisa had

come with Kate in Kate's car. Now they all stood in front of Bruce's house, where they'd agreed to meet.

"You wore *that* outfit to go to a party *not* to flirt?" Lisa scoffed.

"It's the first round of Choose or Lose," Jamie reminded her. "And the question is, can a well-dressed Jamie Dobrin go into a party, say hello to a gorgeous guy, pour herself a Coke, drink the Coke with the guy, and then leave without flirting with him? Choose or Lose."

Kate's dark laugh said it all. "No way. But I'll be there watching, just for the amusement factor."

"I vote no, too," Lisa agreed.

Sara shrugged. "I'm abstaining."

"You can't abstain," Jamie told her.

"I just did."

And inside, I feel like I should be abstaining, too, Jamie thought. *I'm scared. This is my last chance. And I just don't know what's going to happen. But the only failure is not to try.*

"Fine," Jamie said, trying to sound more confident than she felt. "And if I win, I get to ask you all another Choose or Lose. Don't forget."

"Why do I doubt that that will be necessary?" Kate asked dryly.

"Doubt all you want, Kate," Jamie said, her voice steady. "You're wrong."

With a quick turn and a lot of false bravado, she headed up the walkway to Bruce's front door. Her friends had no choice but to follow.

The door was open, and Jamie stepped inside. The place was rocking—people dancing everywhere, the captain of the football team singing karaoke through a microphone along with Li'l Kim. Your basic zoo.

"We'll be watching!" Lisa warned Jamie over the music.

Jamie pushed her way through the crowd, making her way toward where she thought the kitchen should be. Before she found it, someone tapped her on the shoulder.

"Hi," the someone said. A male voice. A male voice she recognized. Drake.

She turned to him and saw her friends over his shoulder. Lisa wiggled her fingers at Jamie, and her eyes said, "You're finished now. You lose!"

Jamie turned to Drake. "Hi." She gulped over the lump in her throat. "Great party, huh?"

"Decent," Drake said to her, his blue eyes looking into hers. "You here alone?"

"With some friends."

"That guy I saw you macking with in the theater?"

Jamie shook her head. "Um, no. He isn't here."

"Bummer." Drake's smile told Jamie he meant just the opposite. "I guess maybe that gives me a chance with the hottest sophomore I've ever seen. Can I get you a drink? A Coke or something?"

And the question is, can I go into that party, say hello to a gorgeous guy, pour myself a Coke, drink the Coke with the guy, and then walk out of the party without flirting with him? Choose or Lose. But did the guy have to be Drake?

"Er, sure," Jamie said. "Love to."

Drake took her hand and led her into the kitchen, where there was a huge spread of food and drink, including a six-foot submarine sandwich. Jamie managed to extricate her hand from his, on the pretext of pushing some hair off her face.

"Great-looking sandwich," Drake said to her. "You want some?"

Jamie wasn't listening. She was at the far end of the kitchen table, pouring herself a Coke. "Hey, pour me one, too," Drake called to her. "We'll toast to getting to know each other better."

Jamie poured two glasses of Coke with shaking hands, afraid that her flirt gene would kick in at any minute. She could see her friends watching her from the other side of the breakfront.

"Lots of ice, okay?" Drake asked her.

"Sure." She handed him his drink.

"A toast," Drake proposed. "To you." He raised his paper cup, indicating that Jamie should raise hers. And all the while, his soft, sexy smile was pulling Jamie into his spell.

They clinked cups. And drank. "Another?" Drake moved closer.

Jamie smiled, her mind wildly searching for some reason to get away from him. "I'd love to . . .

to . . . to . . . toothache! I have the most terrible toothache!"

Drake looked concerned. "Since when?"

"Since now!" Jamie cried, reaching for her jaw. "Oooh, this hurts. So much. Gotta run. See ya!"

She put down her cup, turned on her heels, and fled, leaving a shocked Drake standing in the kitchen. She ran outside, her friends trailing after her. "I did it!" she shouted, jumping up and down on Bruce's front lawn. "I did it! I won Choose or Lose! With Drake! I can do it! I don't have to flirt anymore! And you all watched it happen!"

"Wonders will never cease," Kate said, grinning hugely.

"Amazing," Lisa agreed.

Sara only nodded.

"We're not finished," Jamie reminded them. "That's the first round. But now there's a second."

"Why bother?" Kate asked. "You proved your point."

"I'd like to hear what Jamie is up to," Sara said.

"Okay," Jamie declared. "Choose or Lose, round two. I know that on Sundays you guys usually go to the mall, to hang out at the food court with your boyfriends. Well, tomorrow, instead of doing that, come over to my house at two and we'll work on the 'zine. Blow off the guys and the mall."

All three girls looked unhappy with the challenge.

"Choose or Lose," Jamie told them. "Choose or Lose."

It was five minutes after two. Jamie was all alone in her bedroom. She'd paced across it so many times in the past hour, she had practically worn a path in the carpet.

They didn't come, she thought. *They chose guys over our friendship, and I didn't. But I still feel like I'm the big loser.*

All right, then. She would just have to find a way to go on by herself. Maybe she could make new friends. But it would never be the same as—

"You know, I've always said that you are a really strange girl," Kate said from the doorway.

"Kind of eccentric," Lisa added. "Choosing a 'zine over guys?"

A smile spread over Jamie's face. "You came."

"Now, that's what I call stating the obvious." Kate casually sat on Jamie's bed. She waved a piece of paper in the air. "I worked on an article this morning. For the new and improved *American Grrls.* It needs some editing, though."

"Mine, too," Lisa added, pulling some papers from the back pocket of her jeans. "Actually, I need a lot of editing." They handed their papers to Jamie.

She couldn't stop smiling. "I was so afraid you wouldn't—"

"You really do need to trust your friends more," Kate said blithely.

"Besides, you proved yourself at the party last night," Lisa added. "Frankly, I don't know if I could have resisted Drake."

Jamie bit her lower lip. "I don't suppose you know if Sara is coming?"

Kate shrugged. "We haven't heard from her."

So, Jamie thought, *the only one who can't forgive me is the one I care about the most. And I guess she's also the one I hurt the most.*

Jamie went to the kitchen for a junk-food run, and the three of them got busy planning a new issue of their 'zine. Well, Jamie tried to plan a new issue. But without Sara there, it wasn't nearly the same. There was a giant hole in Jamie's heart, and no way to fill it.

But she tried. An hour later she was hard at work at her computer, laying out Lisa's article, when she felt a tap on her right shoulder.

"Not now," she mumbled, "I'm—"

"Please turn around."

That voice. Sara's.

"Sara!"

"Jamie!"

Kate and Lisa grinned happily at them both.

"You're late," Jamie pointed out.

Sara nodded. "I almost didn't come at all."

Jamie walked over to her. "But you did come. Why?"

Sara pushed some curls behind one ear. "Because I'm an idiot, maybe. You really hurt me, Jam. And I didn't want to get set up to be hurt again."

"I'm so sorry," Jamie whispered.

"Look, we're human, okay?" Kate called over to them. "Can we just admit that and get over all this? And cut each other a little slack?"

"Can we?" Jamie asked Sara.

"I hope," Sara said. "I'll try if you will."

"I believe this is what is known as learning from your mistakes," Kate declared.

"Which, when you think about it," Jamie added, "is an experience much more fun to share than Kate's old bikini."

They thought about that a moment.

"Nah!" they all said at once, and then broke out laughing. The next thing they knew, they were hugging one another so hard it felt as if they would never let go of each other again.

"And I can't believe we almost lost one another," Sara said. "Over guys."

"*So* uncool," the new and improved Lisa pronounced.

"On all our parts," Sara added.

"Thank you," Jamie whispered, choked up.

"One for all—" Kate yelled.

"And all for one!" they shouted, just like they

used to when they were little kids sharing Kate's infamous bikini.

Jamie's heart felt as if it would burst. They had all changed. And they'd continue to change—that was inevitable. But that didn't mean they had to lose one another. Not over guys. Not over anything.

Girl power—*American Grrls* power—could live on.

About the Authors

CHERIE BENNETT and JEFF GOTTESFELD have co-written many well-loved series for teens, including *Teen Angels*, *Sunset Island*, and now *Mirror Image*. Cherie also writes hardcover fiction, including the award-winning *Life in the Fat Lane* and *Zink*. She is also one of America's finest young playwrights (*Anne Frank & Me*; *Searching for David's Heart*), a two-time New Visions/New Voices playwriting winner at the Kennedy Center. Her Copley News Service teen advice column, *Hey Cherie!*, is syndicated nationally. Cherie and Jeff just celebrated their tenth anniversary; they live in Los Angeles and Nashville. Contact them at P.O. Box 150326, Nashville, TN 37215; or send e-mail to authorchik@aol.com.

DARK SECRETS™
by Elizabeth Chandler

Who is Megan? She's about to find out....

#1: Legacy of Lies

Megan thought she knew who she was.

Until she came to Grandmother's house.

Until she met Matt, who angered and attracted her as no boy ever had before.

Then she began having dreams again, of a life she never lived, a love she never knew...a secret that threatened to drive her to the grave.

Home is where the horror is....

#2: Don't Tell

Lauren is coming home, eight years after her mother's mysterious drowning. They said it was an accident. But the tabloids screamed murder. Aunt Jule was her only refuge, the beloved second mother she's returning to see. But first Lauren stops at Wisteria's annual street festival and meets Nick, a tease, a flirt, and a childhood playmate.

The day is almost perfect—until she realizes she's being watched.

A series of nasty "accidents" makes Lauren realize someone wants her dead.

And this time there's no place to run....

Archway Paperbacks
Published by Pocket Books

Beware cheerleaders bearing gifts....

NIGHT OF THE POMPON
by the teen sensation writer
Sarah Jett

Pompons aren't just for
pep rallies any more....

Who knows what evil lies beyond the oven door?
Jendra MacKenzie knows—it's a strangely powerful
pompon that turns bright-eyed cheerleaders into gray-
eyed monsters. But what she doesn't know is how to
explain the unusual events unfolding at the Davy
Crockett school ever since ultra-popular Tina
Shepard handed her a coyote head and made her the
cheerleading mascot. Who's responsible for the sudden disappearance of the last mascot, and the principal's pants...and the principal?

When Jendra searches for answers, she finds nothing
but trouble. Propelled by powers she can't control, she
winds up disco dancing on top of her desk, flying to a
faraway dentist's office, and dodging falling eighth-
graders in the second story girls' bathroom. If this
trend toward the bizarre continues, she might even
pass pre-algebra...unless the cheerleaders have something more sinister in mind....

Archway Paperbacks
Published by Pocket Books

3045

Todd Strasser's

HERE COMES HEAVENLY

Here Comes Heavenly

She just appeared out of nowhere. Spiky purple hair, tons of earrings and rings. Hoops through her eyebrow and nostril, and tattoos on both arms. She said her name was Heavenly Litebody. Our nanny. Nanny???

Dance Magic

Heavenly is cool and punk. She sure isn't the nanny our parents wanted for my baby brother, Tyler. And what's with all those ladybugs?

Pastabilities

Heavenly Litebody goes to Italy with the family and causes all kinds of merriment! But...is the land of *amore* ready for her?

Spell Danger

Kit has to find a way to keep Heavenly Litebody, the Rands' magical, mysterious nanny from leaving the family forever.

Available from Archway Paperbacks
Published by Pocket Books

2307.01

I'm 16,
I'm a witch,
and I still have
to go to school?

Look for a new title
every month
Based on the hit TV series

From Archway Paperbacks
Published by Pocket Books